To Avery + Owen,

All the best!

Gold Medal Threat

A Casey Clark Mystery

by

Michael Balkind

TELEMACHUS PRESS

Reviews

"A great novel, with twists and turns that take the reader on a ride with Casey after he finds himself at the wrong place at the wrong time. Once you start reading, it is hard to put down, with all the excitement that surrounds Casey's quest to stop killers from ruining the Olympics. A book that will have you on the edge of your seat the whole time."
Tim Parker (age 13)

"Gold Medal Threat, was very interesting and hard to put down. It is a perfect book for teens and preteens. It is written exactly how a teenager would think, act, and speak. It's amazing how in this book teens are treated as adults with respect. The story was very suspenseful and mysterious. The crime was a great choice for the setting. I would definitely recommend this book to a friend. It was, without a doubt, one of the best books I have ever read."
Breanna Gardner (age 12)

"This book is very thrilling and filled with suspense, mystery, and action. A great novel for kid mystery fans. Humor is twisted inside every chapter. The author takes you on a journey with many twists and turns. The main characters are likable, smart, funny, and resourceful. I loved every chapter."
Jacob Tabs (age 11)

"Gold Medal Threat is one of those books that puts a big smile on your face and makes your day better. I truly recommend it to everyone, at every age. I bet my grandma would love it too, because you can't dislike a book like this. It's so much fun! I loved it!"
Bianca M. Calin (age 14)

This book is a work of fiction. Names, characters, places and incidents are either the product of the author's imagination or are used fictitiously. Any resemblance to actual persons, living or dead, or to actual events or locales is entirely coincidental.

Cover Designed by Telemachus Press, LLC

Cover Art:
Copyright © 8057424/iStockphoto
Copyright © 2956053/iStockphoto
Copyright © 5939311/iStockphoto
Copyright © 21373182/iStockphoto

Published by Telemachus Press, LLC
http://www.telemachuspress.com

Visit the author website:
http://www.balkindbooks.com

Library of Congress Control Number: 2013930218

ISBN: 978-1-939337-13-9 (eBook)
ISBN: 978-1-939337-44-3 (paperback)

Version 2014.06.12

Printed in the United States of America

10 9 8 7 6 5 4 3 2 1

Acknowledgements

I have many people to thank for helping to bring Gold Medal Threat to fruition ...

Chelsea D'Agostino, my newest editor. Chelsea, your hard work made this novel so much better. I have no doubt that you posses the talent to achieve tremendous success in the writing/editing/publishing world.

Wanda Hartzenberg, my reviewer friend from the other side of the world. Wanda, your insight and suggestions were spot on. Thanks for all your help.

All the wonderful people at Telemachus Press. You make the difficult part of publishing a little easier.

Tim Parker, Samantha Westmoreland, Charlie Weale, Breanna Gardner, Bianca Calin, Jacob Tabs and Earl Miller—Thank you all for your quotes and reviews.

Tim Green, former NFL Defensive End, Attorney, TV & Radio Personality, and New York Times Bestselling Author! Tim, thank you for taking the time during your whirlwind book signing tour of Unstoppable (a book I highly recommend,) to read and write the cover blurb for Gold Medal Threat.

And finally, to my wife, Greer, and my kids, Betsy, Hunter & Reid, thanks for putting up with my non-stop, annoying questions, as I continue to write and edit my books.

Dedications

Uncle George, you were many things to me; intelligent, worldly, a bit intimidating and somewhat mysterious. I wish we'd been able to spend more time together. You are missed.

I also dedicate this novel to all those lost in the devastating Newtown, Connecticut tragedy on 12/14/12. Words cannot express the sadness of such a senseless taking of so many innocent lives.

Charlotte Bacon, Daniel Barden, Rachel Davino, Olivia Engel, Josephine Gay, Ana M. Marquez-Greene, Dylan Hockley, Dawn Hochsprung, Madeleine F. Hsu, Catherine V. Hubbard, Chase Kowalski, Jesse Lewis, James Mattioli, Grace McDonnell, Anne Marie Murphy, Emilie Parker, Jack Pinto, Noah Pozner, Caroline Previdi, Jessica Rekos, Avielle Richman, Lauren Rousseau, Mary Sherlach, Victoria Soto, Benjamin Wheeler, Allison N. Wyatt

Gold Medal Threat

A Casey Clark Mystery

Chapter 1

SHEER EXCITEMENT MIXED with a hint of adrenaline kept Casey and Johnny from getting much sleep on the long flight to Australia. After hours of playing Battlefield, watching *The Simpsons* reruns and eating way too much candy and chips, the boys were beyond fidgety. The huge leather recliners on Casey's dad's jet were very comfortable, but twenty-one hours on any plane is just too much.

"It's hard to believe we've been flying for almost a full day," Casey said quietly, so as not to wake the others.

"I know," Johnny whispered. "And with the time change of sixteen hours, it's like we're flying into the future."

"Yeah, it's like we gain a day and lose a day at the same time," Casey said.

"Huh?" Johnny said with a baffled look.

"Well, if we fly into tomorrow but it takes us a day to … oh, forget it. It's confusing, but it's pretty cool."

"Yeah, and kind of weird, too."

Casey nodded, then turned to stare out the small window at the star-filled sky and quickly became mesmerized. His mind wandered back a couple of months to when his dad had told Johnny and him about coming to the Summer Olympics. As usual, his dad had made coming on the trip dependent on something. This time it was grades. Not that their grades were low; Johnny and Casey were pretty smart. They both got A's in almost all their subjects, except Art for Casey and French for Johnny. But they had both been a little distracted lately. Casey had missed a few easy problems on a math test and Johnny had messed up on an English paper. Mr. Taishoff, Casey's math teacher, told Casey's dad that he was surprised because he was sure Casey knew how to solve the problems. Casey and Johnny both admitted that they had been distracted at the time because they had been helping the AllSport Security team solve a campus crime as part of one of their elective classes. Classes at AllSport were similar to other school's classes except for the electives. Since most of the kids in AllSport's school would live their lives surrounded by sports, the school offered such electives as sports management, sports psychology, sports journalism, and sports TV and film. But, the class that Casey and Johnny loved more than any other was unique to AllSport. It was Sports Criminology.

AllSport, a unique, high-end sports training facility, was the heart of the Inner City Sports Foundation, or ICSF. Casey's dad, Reid Clark, one of the top golfers on the PGA tour, along with his agent and business partner, Buck Green, had started the ICSF years ago and it had since become one of the nation's top charities. Contributors loved the ICSF concept and how it helped at so many levels. ICSF recruited inner-city teens who exhibited the capability to become professional athletes or Olympians and provided the necessary training to help these kids reach their full potential. Many of these same kids, without the help of the ICSF, would have faced the typical problems of the inner city streets: crime, drugs, jail, and occasionally even death. Many of the recruits had been members of violent street gangs and were regularly involved in criminal activity. When ICSF recruiters offered them the AllSport opportunity, they also gave them warnings. Any illicit activity at all, such as drugs or fighting, would cause the end of their AllSport training and opportunity.

AllSport always had a very diverse mix of people on campus. There were the very wealthy contributors to the organization as well as the families and friends of the athletes, most of whom were at the extreme opposite end of the financial scale. At times, this combination had proven to be extremely volatile.

Years before Casey was born, his dad had received a death threat while playing in the Masters tournament. Private Investigator, Jay Scott, and his team were hired to find the perpetrator before harm came to Mr. Clark. Casey vividly remembered that when he had originally heard the story of how his dad had been shot while playing in a golf tournament, he had been both upset and intrigued at the same time. Obviously his dad had not been killed, otherwise there would be no Casey Clark. Reid Clark had been golfing that day wearing a vest of Zylon body armor. Casey remembered hearing the story and immediately Googled the word Zylon. After all, every mystery he had read said that bullet proof vests were made of Kevlar. Zylon, it turned out, was a lighter, more flexible material than Kevlar. Although it had been proven to be less safe, it was offered to Reid as an alternative, because playing in a golf tournament while wearing a heavy Kevlar vest would be almost impossible.

The death threat and attempt on his dad's life had been the first of many crimes that had occurred involving AllSport. In fact, it had become somewhat of a not-so-funny campus joke that murder, kidnapping, and extortion were just three of the many sports found at AllSport. It seemed the formula that created AllSport's success was also a recipe for disaster. As AllSport had grown, so had its security team, lead by Jay Scott, Joel Rebah and Stu Mann. These men were as good at their game as Casey's dad was at golf. They all had been Navy SEALs. Each had black belts in various styles of martial arts and was an expert in all kinds of weaponry.

Working at AllSport for them was fun, exciting and very stimulating. And, as they had described to Casey, it kept them sharp, both mentally and physically. Furthermore, they had all become part of the Clark extended family and each felt it was their duty to protect the Clarks at all costs. Each of these men, as well as Buck Green, had become Casey's non-blood "uncles."

As close as Casey had become with his "uncles," he was even closer with Johnny Rebah, Joel's son. Casey and Johnny were only half a year apart in age and had grown up together at AllSport. As best friends often are, they were similar in many ways. They both loved sports, yet neither of them had the goods to pursue any sport professionally. They both really enjoyed martial arts and were regularly taught by some of the best trainers in the art, namely Joel and Stu, who both had been martial arts instructors in the Navy SEALs.

Casey and Johnny were lucky kids. They lived in a community filled with professional athletes, traveled often around the world with their parents to all kinds of big events, and most importantly, had each other to hang out with and watch each other's back.

**

Turbulence caused the plane to shake and snapped Casey from his thoughts. He reached up and rubbed his face. A face adored by many young girls at AllSport and around the world. Casey's looks were a mixture of the best parts of each of his parents. His dad, at one time, had actually been named *Celeb Magazine's* sexiest man of the year. His mom, Shane, was also a stunner. Casey had his mom's dark complexion and his dad's wavy, dirty-blond hair and crystal blue eyes. He was five feet, eight inches tall and fairly thin for his height. Paparazzi were always snapping pictures of the three of them for magazine articles and covers. Television cameras zoomed in on them at celebrity events and after each golf tournament that Reid won. The world had watched Casey grow up.

Casey looked around to see if any of the others had been woken by the turbulence. Sitting in the other plush, brown leather, reclining seats were Casey's mom, Shane, Johnny's mom, Cindy Rebah, Reid's agent and business partner Buck Green, Chief of Security, Jay Scott, and two other body guards.

Casey's dad, Reid Clark, had flown to Australia two weeks earlier to practice with the rest of the United States Olympic Golf Team. Reid's body guards, Joel Rebah and Stu Mann, as well as his caddie, Buddy, had gone with him.

**

During their first day in Australia, Casey and Johnny spent their time wandering through the Olympic Village. They saw many professional athletes and celebrities that they had previously met at AllSport. Johnny began to roll his green eyes and make fun of Casey whenever a girl around their age recognized Casey. Some of the girls stared, some of them whispered to their friends, and some of them pointed from a distance. One girl approached Casey and said, "Oh my God, you're Casey Clark."

Johnny laughed after the girl walked away and said, "Duh! Like you don't know who you are."

"Whatever," Casey said, trying to hide his embarrassment. "She was kind of cute."

"No, she wasn't. She was *beautiful!* You are so lucky."

"Lucky? I get so nervous. I never know what to say."

"Try this." Johnny quickly jumped out in front of Casey and put his hand out to shake Casey's. "Hi, it's nice to meet you. What's your name?"

Casey laughed. "Oh shut up, you idiot," he said as he pushed Johnny aside and kept walking. "I'm hungry. Let's get something to eat."

They looked up and down the street at all the stores and restaurants. "What's Hungry Jacks?" Johnny asked. "It looks like Burger King, even the logo is the same."

"I don't know, but it looks like Burger King and it smells like Burger King. Let's go try it."

They walked across the street and entered the busy eatery. Immediately after eating they both admitted to being very tired. The jet lag and time change were getting to them. They went back to their room in the hotel, turned on the TV, and both quickly fell asleep.

Casey was awakened by the ringing of the phone at six p.m. He picked it up and mumbled, "Hello?"

"Hi Casey, it's Mom. Are you boys ready to get some dinner?"

Casey looked over at Johnny lying on the other bed fully clothed and snoring. "We ate lunch and then came back here and just kinda passed out. Johnny is still sleeping and I'm still really tired, Mom. I think we'll skip dinner and just sleep. Okay?"

"Of course, sweetheart. We'll talk in the morning. Dad really wants to see you."

"Tell him I'm really sorry. I'll see you both in the morning. I love you."

"Love you too, honey. Sleep well."

He hung up the phone, rolled over, and fell back to sleep.

**

Casey awoke and turned to look at the clock: 3:42 a.m. He yawned loudly.

"Hey, it's about time you woke up. I've been awake since three. I wonder how long it will take us to get used to the time change."

"We'll probably get used to it just as we have to leave," Casey said before yawning again.

Johnny picked up the remote and turned on the TV. He clicked through a bunch of channels. "There's nothing good on. You want to go downstairs and check out the gym?"

"You think it's open?"

"I don't know. Let's go find out."

They got up and changed into shorts and t-shirts.

The hallway was brightly lit but eerily quiet. "This is kinda weird, huh?" Johnny whispered.

"Yeah, like that saying, the lights are on but nobody's home."

"It reminds me of that scary movie we saw a couple of years ago. What was it called? You know, the one where the kid is walking through the empty halls of the big hotel."

"The Shining?"

"Yeah, that's it," Johnny said with a visible shudder.

"Redrum," whispered Casey.

"Huh?"

"That's what the kid kept saying. Redrum, redrum. It's murder spelled backwards."

"Oh yeah, redrum," Johnny repeated a little too loudly.

"Shh."

"Oh right. Sorry!" he said at full volume.

"Will you be quiet?" whispered Casey.

Johnny covered his mouth with his hand and laughed quietly.

They rode the elevator down to the basement level and walked to the gym entrance. Casey put his hotel keycard in the slot and they both smiled when they heard a quiet click and saw the tiny light turn green on the mechanism. Johnny pulled the heavy glass door open and they entered the dark room.

"You look on that side for the light switch and I'll look over here," Casey said.

Just as Casey found and flipped the light switch he heard a loud thud coming from Johnny's direction. A quick look, just as the fluorescent lights flickered to life, revealed Johnny lying on the floor next to a weight rack.

"Ow," Johnny moaned.

"You okay?" Casey asked.

"No. I stepped on a dumbbell that some idiot didn't put back on the rack."

Casey laughed.

"You think it's funny?" Johnny asked, holding the side of his head.

"Kind of," Casey said, grinning.

"Glad I could make you laugh, jerk," Johnny said, wincing in pain.

"Do you need help getting up?" Casey said, picking up the weight and placing it in its proper spot.

"No thanks. I hit my head on something when I fell but it's not that bad."

"Lucky it was your head. It's hard to damage a rock!" Casey said, grinning.

"Ha ha, very funny."

Casey smiled and helped Johnny get up. "Where did you hit your head?"

"Right here." Johnny pointed above his right temple.

Casey looked at Johnny's head. His fair skin and short buzz cut of brown hair made it easy to see his scalp. "Well, there's no blood."

"I'm fine. Let's check this place out and get in a workout. We haven't done anything physical in days. I don't want to get soft."

"You, soft? No way! You're all bones!"

"Go ahead, make all the fun of me you want. I'll kick your butt any day."

Casey shrugged. Johnny was right. Even though Casey was a little taller, Johnny beat him every time they wrestled or fought in any type of martial arts exercise. Casey was no match for Johnny's more muscular frame.

Casey began walking around and checking out the exercise machines. One room contained treadmills, bikes and other cardiovascular machines. Another room had all the weight lifting equipment. The entire floor of the third room was lined with mats. The equipment wasn't quite as up to date as AllSport's, but it would do. Casey sat on a mat and started to stretch. Johnny joined him on another mat. After about five minutes of stretching they hit the weights and worked out for a while. Then Casey said, "You want to spar a little?"

"Sure," Johnny said. They went back to the room with the mats and practiced their karate for about fifteen minutes.

"I gotta pee. Where's the bathroom?" Casey asked.

"There're entrances to the locker rooms in the weight room and the cardio room," Johnny said. "I'll come with you. I want to see if I can find something for my headache."

"Is it from hitting your head before?"

"I don't know. I really didn't feel anything then, but it started to hurt when we were lifting weights."

"The lifting probably increased the blood pressure in your head."

"Maybe. All I know is it really hurts now."

They walked into the locker room and while Casey headed for the toilets, Johnny went to the area where the sinks were lined up and looked through the various drawers and jars for some kind of pain reliever.

"Find anything?" Casey asked as he entered and washed his hands.

"Nah, it's probably against the law to leave any kind of drugs out in public."

"Advil isn't a drug." He held up his palm stopping Johnny, just as he was about to talk. "Don't even say it. Of course I know it's a drug. And of course you know what I meant. So, just shut-up."

Johnny smiled. "You know me way too well!"

"Yeah, and you know me pretty good too."

Johnny looked at Casey and smiled. "I guess I do."

Casey grinned and nodded softly. "You want to go find something for your headache or you want to keep working out?"

Johnny looked up at the clock. "It's still only 4:30. How about thirty minutes on the treadmill?"

"Sounds good to me."

They walked back into the weight room and heard voices along with the sound of a treadmill. They immediately hushed and looked at each other with frowns. They liked having the gym to themselves. Then, just as they were about to turn the corner and walk from the weight area into the cardio room they heard something that made them stop dead in their tracks. The discussion between a man and a woman was just audible over the noise of the treadmills.

"Why don't we just take her out?" the woman said.

"Take her out? You really want to kill her?" said the man.

Johnny and Casey look at each other, wide eyed.

"Kidnapping her is much too risky. You remember the job in Peru? We almost got caught because we kidnapped the guy instead of just killing him. If we get caught here, it's jail for life."

"More likely, the death penalty."

"Nah, there's no capital punishment here and besides, we won't get caught," the woman said. "We just need a plan."

"I don't know. We're not making enough on this job to risk it. And besides, we don't know how they'll feel about it."

"How they'll feel? Are you kidding me? You think they'll care how we deal with this? No way! They only said to make sure she doesn't compete. They didn't say how we should do it. And be-sides, the people who hire us know exactly what we do. They hired us for this job because we have a reputation for getting things done. The only thing they care about is securing a gymnastics medal for the boss's niece."

"You're probably right, but I just don't like the idea of killing a kid. Kidnapping was one thing. Murder is a different story. It's just ... it's wrong."

"Since when did you get so sentimental?" she asked.

"Are you going to tell me that killing an innocent kid doesn't bother you at all?"

"Look, I didn't get into this business for sentimental reasons. It's all about the money. With the money from this job and maybe one or two more we can retire."

"Yeah, I guess. I just can't believe the thought of killing a kid doesn't bother you."

She laughed.

"What's so funny?" he asked.

"Honey, for the right amount of money I might be willing to kill *you*."

"I guess I better start watching my back."

"Nah. I don't think you have to worry about it. I haven't done it yet and if the three million that you have on your head now hasn't enticed me, chances are nobody is going to top that offer."

"That's very sweet of you, dear. I'm glad I'm worth more to you than a few mil."

"You know I love you, babe. I wouldn't kill you for anything less than five million."

"Well, aren't I just the luckiest guy?"

Casey and Johnny turned and stared at each other with bulging eyes. Johnny motioned with a quick point to the door that they should get out of there now. Casey put his finger to his lips to make sure Johnny stayed quiet, then held it up in the air asking for one more minute.

The man and woman continued talking.

"So?" the woman said.

The man sighed, "I'll admit, it'll be faster and easier to just kill her."

"So, it's settled then. Let's go up to the room and make a plan."

Johnny reached for Casey's arm and tugged, mouthing, "Let's go!"

While Casey knew Johnny was right, he stayed where he was for a moment, thinking. While he was scared out of his mind, something in him wanted to get a look at the man and woman. He turned and looked quickly at Johnny, who was already halfway to the exit. Johnny gave him a pleading look and waved his arm frantically, begging Casey to follow.

Casey took a step towards Johnny then stopped and motioned for Johnny to go. He then turned, took a deep breath, slowly let it out, took one more second to build his nerve and walked into the cardio room. Just as he entered, he saw the back of the woman as she walked from the gym through the entrance to the ladies locker room. Her dark, shoulder length ponytail swung as she turned and walked behind the closing door.

The man was nowhere in sight, but as Casey quickly looked at the men's locker room door, he heard its lock click as it closed.

Still scared, Casey hesitated. *Should I follow him into the locker room?* He wondered. As much as he wanted to see who the guy was, he was dealing with cold-blooded killers. He could describe the woman from behind, but if he could identify the man, it would be a big help. Casey's heart was racing as he walked toward the locker room door. He reached for the handle, took another deep breath, opened the door and entered. There was no one near the rows of metal lockers and wooden benches. Casey walked past them and peeked into the shower area. Nobody was there and there was no sound of running water. He walked further, past the toilets and then the sinks. The bathroom was empty. Where could the guy have gone? Then, as he walked back to the locker area he heard the sound of a door closing somewhere on the other side of the room. He followed the sound to another door.

He slowly pushed it open and looked out into a hallway. He heard the unmistakable ding of an elevator bell and quickly walked toward it. He turned the corner just in time to see the heel of a blue running shoe as it entered the elevator down the hall. Casey pushed his fear aside and ran, but the elevator shut before he reached it.

He hadn't realized until then that besides his heart racing, he was also hyperventilating. He stood there, trying to calm down, wondering what he should do next. What he and Johnny had just overheard was devastating. Someone, some Olympic athlete, was going to be murdered. *But who? ... And by whom?*

Casey started to walk back to the locker room and heard the ding of the elevator bell again. He turned back and looked up to see a red number twelve on the elevator's digital readout. He turned again and began walking quickly back towards the locker room. Then, after another quick thought, he began looking for an entrance to the women's locker room. Similar to the men's, the women's locker room should have a hallway entrance too. He turned a corner and there it was, just being opened by someone from the inside.

Casey's heart raced faster as he watched a woman with lots of make-up walk out with a bag slung over her shoulder and a water bottle in her hand. Her build was similar to the woman's in the gym. She smiled and said, "Bonjour," as she walked by. Casey turned and watched her walk down the hall, noticing as she reached up with her free hand to push her blond hair from her face. He sighed and thought, *blond hair and she speaks French—nope, it's not her.*

He stayed where he was with his eyes glued to the women's locker room door for a few more minutes, hoping that she'd walk out. Then, he thought about what it would look like to her if she walked out and there was a boy standing there, staring at her. *She'd probably think I'm a freak.* He quickly looked around for a seat or a bench and a newspaper within view of the door. Nope, just an empty hallway. He was nervous and not sure what else to do, so he walked back to the elevator.

Both his heart and his mind raced as he rode up to the top floor. *Will Johnny be in our room,* he thought, *or will he have already gone to Uncle Joel's room to tell him? I hope he's waiting for me in our room. We have to figure out what to do next.* "Oh my God," he mumbled to himself as he reached up and put his hand over his heart. It was beating a million miles an hour. *I have to calm down,* he thought. *Oh sure, calm down. I just overheard two killers talking about murdering an Olympic athlete and I'm supposed to calm down.* The ding of the elevator made Casey jump and kind of brought him to his senses. The walk to his room from the elevator seemed very long. As he got close, he searched his pockets for his keycard. He couldn't find it. He must have left it in the gym. *Oh, man. This is just great. I'm not going back down there to look for it. I'll just get another one from the front desk later.* Just as he was passing his parent's suite, their door was opening. Casey's first thought was to hide. He wasn't ready to tell anybody about the problem yet. As he quickened his pace to get to his room, he heard his father's hushed voice, "Casey, is that you? Why are you up so early?"

Casey turned around. "Hey, Dad." He walked toward his father, still not sure of what to say or not to say.

"Hurry up," whispered his dad. "I've missed you. I want a hug."

Casey hurried into his father's outstretched arms and they hugged. Casey closed his eyes and held tight. A little too tight and for a little too long. His dad's hug felt good. It always helped assure Casey that everything was okay. Well, in this case, almost okay was good enough.

"What's wrong, son?" his father asked quietly.

"Dad, we just heard a man and a woman talk about killing somebody."

"*What?* Who is we?"

"Me and Johnny. We couldn't sleep, so we went down to the gym."

"Where's Johnny now? How come he's not with you?"

"I hope he's in our room. Let's go see and we'll tell you everything. It's crazy dad! These people are hired killers. You need to get Uncle Joel and Stu and Jay. You all need to hear about this." Casey was still in a panic but talking about it, especially to his dad, was making him feel much better.

"It's only 5:40. Do I really need to wake them? Why don't you just tell me, for now?"

"*Dad!* Did you hear what I said? They're assassins and they're going to kill someone."

"Okay, okay. I'll round them up. What room are you in? I'm sure your mother told me, but I forgot."

"It's right here," Casey said, pointing to the next door. "It's 722. Hurry, Dad. Get them up."

"Alright, let's go in and I'll use your phone. There's no need to bother your mother with this."

Casey knocked quietly on his door and waited.

"Where's your key?" his dad asked.

"I don't know. I must have left it somewhere down in the gym. It got a little crazy down there."

"What do you mean, crazy?"

"I'll tell you everything when we get in the room." Casey knocked again. "Johnny, open up. It's me." He said quietly through the door.

Finally, the door opened. "Sorry," said Johnny. "I was in the bathroom splashing cold water on my face. Thank God you're alive. I kept thinking that they got you. I was pretty freaked out. I didn't know what to do."

When Reid entered the room after Casey, Johnny was surprised. "Uncle Reid, I didn't see you there."

"Johnny, what do you mean, you thought they got him? What happened down there?"

"It's okay, Dad, I'm fine. Can you just get everyone in here so we can explain what happened?"

Reid walked to the phone without saying another word. He picked it up and asked the front desk to put him through to Joel's, then Jay's, then Stu's rooms. Without much of an explanation he made it perfectly clear that each of them needed to get to the kids' room immediately.

The men were all staying in the adjoining rooms and were each at the door within minutes. They all entered with very curious looks on their faces.

"What the heck is going on, Reid?" asked Jay Scott. "What could possibly be important enough to wake us all this early?"

"Sit down, gentlemen," said Reid. "The boys seem to have stumbled across a potentially serious situation. Let them explain."

Jay and Reid sat in the armchairs at the small round table in the corner. Stu and Joel sat on the edge of Johnny's bed. Johnny sat on Casey's bed and Casey stood and paced. He still couldn't calm down enough to sit.

"So, who's going to tell us what's going on?" Joel asked.

Johnny pointed at Casey. "Go ahead."

"Okay," Casey said. "I'll try to make this quick. Johnny and I couldn't sleep so we went down to the gym at around four o'clock. After working out for a while we went to the bathroom. Then, when we came out we heard voices. It was a man and a woman who were talking while they were running on treadmills. They had no idea we were there. Obviously, they thought they had the gym to themselves because they started talking about killing someone."

"Killing someone?" blurted Joel.

"Yeah, that's why we asked dad to wake you guys. These people are hired assassins."

"Assassins?" It was Stu's turn to be surprised.

"Yeah, assassins. Right, Johnny?"

Johnny gave a wide-eyed nod.

"Okay, Casey," Jay said. "Calm down and slowly tell us everything you heard."

Casey rubbed his face with both hands. "Oh my God. Let's see. First, the woman said it would be easier and faster to kill her than it would be to kidnap her."

"Do you know who they were talking about?" Jay asked.

"No. But, it's got to be a gymnast because they said that they were being paid to prevent her from competing so that the boss's niece could get a medal in gymnastics."

"A gymnast, huh? There are an awful lot of gymnasts," Reid said.

"Yeah, but we can probably narrow it down to the top few from each country in each category," Jay said.

They all nodded.

"Casey, you mentioned a boss. Whose boss?" Joel asked.

"It kind of sounded like they meant a mafia boss, but I don't know," Casey said.

"Oh, great. Here we go again," Jay said.

The others knew what Jay meant. He was thinking about the mob's involvement in many of their past investigations. Mafia involvement usually made things more difficult.

"Sorry for interrupting, Casey. Please continue."

"Okay." Casey thought for a second before continuing. "The man said that he didn't like the idea of killing a kid. But, the woman said it would be easier and faster than kidnapping, and that there was less chance of them getting caught."

The men nodded as if they agreed.

"She also said something about a job they did in … in … I can't remember."

"Peru," Johnny said.

"Right. It was Peru. She talked about almost getting caught there, because they kidnapped a guy instead of killing him."

Jay looked questioningly at Joel and Stu. They both looked back at him. Joel shook his head and Stu shrugged. Obviously, the Peru story didn't ring a bell with any of them.

"What was said next, Casey?" Jay asked.

"After that, the man asked the woman if killing a kid would bother her at all. She said that she was in it for the money and that there was no room for feelings."

Casey stopped for a second and just looked at the men.

"Is that it? Can you tell us any more?"

"That's pretty much it, right Johnny? Did I miss anything?"

"I don't think so," Johnny said. "That's all I remember."

"Casey, I have a question for you," Reid said. "Why did you come up here after Johnny did? Johnny was already in the room when I saw you in the hallway."

Casey didn't answer. He just looked over at Johnny who also stayed silent.

"Well?" Reid asked.

"You're not going to like this, Dad," Casey said. "I tried to get a look at them."

"Oh no," Reid said with a sigh.

"Don't worry, nothing happened. They didn't see me."

"That's a relief. Do me a favor, Casey. Don't take any more chances."

"I won't."

"Did you see them at all, Casey?" Jay asked.

"Just a little. I saw the woman's back as she walked into the lady's locker room. She was about this tall." He held his hand up to about five and a half feet. "She was kind of thin and had a shoulder length, dark ponytail."

"That's good. Anything else?" asked Jay.

"Well, I tried to follow the man, but I kept missing him. He was in the locker room, but when I entered, he left through a different door. I followed him around a corner and finally saw him just as he was getting on the elevator, but I only saw his foot. He was wearing sneakers."

"Can you remember what kind?"

"It was blue. A running shoe. But no, I didn't see what brand."

"Okay, good job, Casey. At least we have something to go on."

"Oh yeah, one more thing. I'm pretty sure the guy took the elevator up to the twelfth floor."

"Pretty sure?" Jay asked.

"Uncle Jay, I wasn't exactly thinking straight. I don't know if it made stops before it got to the twelfth floor. All I know is that I heard the bell and when I looked up at the floor number thing, there was a twelve."

"Okay, Casey. That's great. I didn't mean to question your judgment. I just needed to understand what you meant."

Casey nodded. "That's okay. It's just that this whole thing has kind of freaked me out."

"I'll bet it has."

Casey's dad walked over and gave him a hug. "Are you okay?"

"Yeah, I am. To tell you the truth, now that I'm with you guys, it's actually getting kind of exciting. I mean, it's scary to think that there are killers at the Olympics, but it's pretty cool to think that we might be able to stop them and save someone's life." Casey looked at Johnny. "Are you doing alright?"

"I guess I feel the same as you. Kind of scared and excited at the same time."

Joel stood, walked over to his son and hugged him.

"Well boys," Jay said. "I know better at this point than to ask you to leave this case up to us. I know you're both very capable and smart, but I want you to be really careful and keep me informed about anything you see or hear. And, if there's even a hint of trouble, I want you to call my cell immediately, okay?"

Casey nodded.

"I have one last question for you two," Jay added.

They both looked at him and raised their brows.

"I'm going to guess that the man and woman spoke English with an American accent. Otherwise, you probably would have mentioned their foreign accent. Am I right?"

"Oh … yeah," Casey said. "I never even thought about that. They both sounded like Americans. I guess I better sharpen my investigative skills if we're going to solve this case, huh."

Reid shook his head. "Will you all please do me a favor? Don't tell Shane or Cindy about the boys helping with this. At least, not yet. It'll just get them all worked up and I can't afford the distraction right now. I have to spend my time on the golf course."

"Reid, don't worry about the boys," Jay said. "I'll make sure they stay out of trouble." He turned to Joel and Stu. "You're both going to need to stick with Reid until we find these people. The less I have to worry about him, the faster I'll be able to take care of this situation." Then he turned toward the boys. "I'm going to go speak with the Olympic Committee now. Please don't go far. And please check in with me every couple of hours. Okay?"

Johnny nodded.

"Alright," agreed Casey with a nod.

"One last thing," Jay said. "I need you all to keep quiet about this. Until we know more, I don't want this couple to know we're looking for them. They are more likely to make mistakes as long as they don't think anyone knows about their mission. And obviously, if word of this gets out to the public, there will be complete chaos here, within hours. That would be a disaster."

Everyone nodded their agreement and the men left the room.

Chapter 2

CASEY SAT ON his bed, looked at Johnny and said, "How do you feel?"

"I'm not sure."

"Me either. I feel lots of things at the same time and all of a sudden I'm really tired."

"Yeah, me too."

"But, I can't sleep. Can you?"

"Nope, I'm too excited."

"Yeah, me too. And I'm also a little scared," Casey admitted.

"Me too."

"So, what do we do now?"

"I don't know. I think Uncle Jay wanted us to stay here," Johnny said.

"No, he just said that we should be careful and report in if we see or hear anything. I can't sit here, I'm too jumpy. Let's go."

"Where?"

"Up to the twelfth floor."

"What? Are you crazy? What are we going to do if we see them?"

"I don't know, but I can't just sit here and wait. Somebody's life is at stake and we may be the only ones who can help. C'mon, let's go."

Johnny slowly stood while shaking his head. "This is crazy!"

"Would you rather sit here and find out that someone got killed?"

"Of course not. I think it's nuts, but I'll come. Can we go get something to eat first?"

"How could you be hungry with all this going on?"

"You know me, I'm always hungry."

"Okay, we'll go down and eat first."

They walked out to the hallway and towards the elevator. Casey pushed the button. After a quick wait, the bell dinged and the doors opened. There were two women and a man facing the boys. Casey's heart skipped a beat when he saw one of the women had a dark, shoulder-length ponytail and was about the same height and build as the woman he saw downstairs. He and Johnny entered and turned to face the door. Casey's heart was racing again. He looked down at the floor and shifted his eyes attempting to look back at the man's feet. No luck. He couldn't see them and turning would be way too obvious. *Is it them?* He thought. *Oh my God.* He tried to control his breathing. The elevator opened and the boys walked into the lobby. Casey moved quickly toward the crowded sitting area and turned to look back.

"Where are they?" he asked.

"Where are who? C'mon, the restaurant is this way," Johnny said pointing.

"Just wait," Casey said quietly. "I'm looking for the people who were on the elevator with us."

"Why? Wait, you think it was them?" Johnny turned to help look.

The lobby was very busy. There were lines of people at the registration desk and brass luggage carts piled high with suitcases being wheeled towards the elevators.

"Is that them?" Johnny asked.

"Where?"

"Over there," Johnny pointed. "Coming out of the gift shop."

"The blond woman?"

"No, the one in front of her," Johnny said. "The woman in the dark blue t-shirt and the guy in shorts."

Casey saw them and his eyes shot down to the guy's feet. His shoes were brown. "He's not wearing sneakers, but he could have changed. Oh, I don't know. This is going to drive me crazy. Let's just go eat."

Johnny nodded and they headed for the restaurant.

The boys' mothers were sitting at a table drinking coffee. "Hi boys," said Cindy Rebah, as they approached.

"Hi, Mom," Johnny said before giving her a hug while Casey hugged his mom.

"Why don't you grab some chairs from another table and join us," Shane said.

They dragged over a couple of chairs and sat.

"So, did you guys catch up on your sleep?" Casey's mom asked.

The boys looked at each other awkwardly.

"What's with the faces?" Johnny's mom asked.

"Uh, we went to sleep really early but then we woke up in the middle of the night and couldn't fall back to sleep," Casey said.

"So, how's Australian late night TV?" Casey's mom asked.

"Bad enough that we went downstairs and worked out in the gym," Casey said.

"In the middle of the night? I'm surprised it was open."

"Yeah, we were too."

"You two didn't spar did you? You have no pads here. You know we hate it when you practice your karate without protection."

"Actually, we fought a little MMA style," Casey said.

Shane Clark's eyes lit up. "You did what?"

"What the heck is MMA?" Johnny's mom asked.

"It's Mixed Martial Arts and it's absolutely crazy. Tell me you're joking, Casey."

Casey didn't answer right away. He shifted his gaze from his mother over to Johnny, then to Mrs. Rebah and then back to his mom. "MMA is awesome, Mom. Johnny and I figure we'll be good enough to get on TV in about two or three years."

"Get outta here. Are you serious?"

Casey nodded.

She looked at Johnny. "Johnny, is he pulling my leg?"

Johnny just looked at her and his mother and finally he broke out in a big smile and started laughing. Casey laughed also.

"You're kidding! Thank God! You really had me going there."

"You really think we'd fight MMA? No way. Those guys are nuts. They're cool to watch, but getting in the ring with them? Unh uh! We'll stick with one martial art at a time, right Johnny?"

Johnny shrugged.

Cindy Rebah said, "Oh, no, Johnny. Maybe I've never seen it, but after hearing Shane and Casey's reaction, you're not getting in one of those rings, young man!"

"Calm down, Ma. It's not like I'm doing it soon."

"Try never."

"Can we just drop it for now, I'm really hungry," Johnny said.

"Fine, we'll drop it for now, but your dad is going to hear about this."

Johnny smiled.

"Why are you smiling? Oh, don't tell me your dad likes this MMA stuff, too."

"Okay, I won't tell you."

Cindy shook her head and looked at Shane. "Do you believe what I have to deal with?"

"You do have your hands full," Shane said. Then she looked at the boys. "Why don't you two go on up to the buffet?"

Casey and Johnny left and came back with plates piled high. They sat and dug in. Casey's eyes roamed the room and whenever men walked past the table he found himself looking down at their feet.

"Did you drop something, Casey?" his mother asked.

"No."

"Then why do you keep looking down at the floor?"

"Uh, I'm looking at sneakers, Mom."

Johnny flinched.

"Why? Do you need new ones? I just got you a pair about a month ago."

"Nah, I just saw some cool ones earlier. They had Olympic rings on them."

"I'm sure you did. Sneakers, shirts, hats, shorts, they have everything. I even saw logoed socks for sale yesterday."

"What, no underwear?" Casey kidded.

"I won't be surprised if we see them for sale too," said his mom with a grin. "So, what are your plans for today, boys? I don't suppose we could talk you into touring some of the venues with us, could we?"

"Maybe this afternoon," Casey said. "I don't think you want to go where we're heading this morning."

"Martial arts, huh?" asked Cindy.

"Yup," Johnny said.

"Aye yi yi," Shane said, shaking her head. "Well, keep your phones turned on in case we need you."

Casey nodded.

"How about we meet for lunch at around," Shane looked at her watch. "Let's say one o'clock, alright? I'll call you at 12:30 and we'll pick a place to meet."

"Sounds good," Casey said. "See ya later."

"Have fun," said Cindy. "And Johnny, promise me you'll stay out of that ring."

"Yeah Mom, like there's a chance I could get in the ring. These are the Olympics, not the gym at AllSport."

"I know. But, I also know *you*, dear."

"Don't worry. I'm not gonna fight an Olympian. I'd get my butt kicked in like a minute. Bye, Mom." He gave her a quick hug and waited while Casey did the same to his mom. Then, they turned and left the restaurant.

"So, do you still want to go up to the twelfth floor or just head out to the martial arts venue?" Johnny asked.

"Martial arts? We're not really going there. That was just your mom's guess."

"I know but it's a great idea. I definitely want to check it out."

"Me too, but we have more important things to do first."

**

"What do we do if we see them?" Johnny asked nervously, as the elevator passed the second floor.

Casey chuckled. "I don't know."

"You think that's funny?"

"No, not really."

"Good, I was beginning to think you were losing your mind. It's one thing when we're back at AllSport trying to figure out who stole a trophy, but this is different. Totally different! Now we're trying to find killers. I think we should wait until Uncle Jay gets back."

"Johnny, if you don't want to go, you don't have to. It's not like I'm forcing you with a gun to your head."

Johnny rolled his eyes. "Was *that* supposed to be funny?"

"Yeah, kind of. Guess not, huh?"

"No. Not at all."

"Okay, whatever. Look, these people are going to kill an Olympic athlete and you and I are the only ones who may be able to identify them. Now, I have no idea how this is going to work out, but I'm going up to the twelfth floor to look around. If you want to come, come. If you don't, that's okay. Push the button for our floor and I'll meet you back in the room in a little while."

Johnny looked at him for a second without moving. "You know, I hate when you do this kind of stuff. You tell me I have a choice when I really don't. If I don't come with you, we'll both know that I'm a chicken. If I do come with you, we may save someone's life or we might get killed ourselves. I'm comin' with you." Johnny turned to face the elevator door and mumbled, "I must be crazy."

Casey smiled.

The elevator stopped on the eighth floor and the doors opened. A tall man and woman were facing the boys about to board the elevator. As the man took a step toward them, the woman asked, "Are you going down?"

"No, up," Casey said.

The man backed up, the doors closed, and the elevator started moving again.

"Oh my God. Did you see that?" Johnny asked in excitement.

"See what?"

"His sneakers! He was wearing blue running shoes! And she … she had a ponytail!"

"He was? She did? I guess I only looked at their faces. I have been looking at every man's feet since this morning and the first ones that I miss are in blue running shoes." He shook his head. "I think she was taller than the woman we're looking for, anyway."

"She was wearing high heels."

"Really? How could I miss all that?"

"You were talking to them while I was looking."

"Wow. High heels, huh? You think it was them?"

Johnny shrugged.

"Should we go follow them?"

"I don't know?"

The elevator stopped on the twelfth floor and the doors opened. Johnny looked at Casey, waiting for his decision.

"Let's go see if we can find them. If not, we'll come back up."

Johnny shrugged again. "Okay," he said, pushing the lobby button on the panel.

Now, because they had a mission, the elevator ride seemed to take forever. It stopped at three floors picking up people at each. The elevator was full. When it stopped on the fourth floor, the doors opened, the people who had been waiting looked skeptically at the crowd, but instead of waiting for the next elevator, they rudely squeezed in. Everyone took a step back except Casey and Johnny who were now pressed up against the rear wall. Casey heard an unmistakable sound come from Johnny. They looked at each other and Johnny raised his brow and made a face confirming Casey's questioning look. They both started giggling.

The ding of the elevator reaching the lobby couldn't have been more welcome. The crowd cleared out of the elevator pretty fast and the boys walked out, cracking up. The looks that they got from some of the people that were in the elevator made them laugh even harder.

"Did you see that woman next to me?" Johnny asked between laughing fits. "I thought her eyes were going to pop out of her head."

"No," said Casey, bending over in laughter. "But, I think the guy in front of you held his breath from the fourth floor all the way to the lobby. His face was bright red when he walked out."

The boys realized they were creating a spectacle of themselves and did their best to calm down. Once they finally both stopped laughing and caught their breath, Casey said, "It's too crowded in here. Let's go outside and watch the entrance for a little while. We'll see if they come or go. If they leave, we'll follow them."

"Yeah, then what?"

"I don't really know yet. Let's just go. They're probably gone already anyway."

They made their way through the busy lobby and exited through the huge automatic revolving doors into the bright sunshine. Squinting, Casey looked at Johnny, "I guess we should have brought our hats or sunglasses."

"You want me to go get them?"

"Nah, it'll take too long. I don't want to miss them if they come out soon. And I really don't want to follow them by myself."

"Okay. We can watch the door from that bench over there," Johnny said, pointing.

"Good."

They hustled toward the bench, but just before they reached it, a couple sat down and unfolded a big map leaving no room for the boys.

Johnny shot Casey a quick, annoyed look. Casey shrugged and pointed toward the four-foot high concrete wall behind the bench. They walked over and with a little effort hoisted themselves up and sat on the edge. "Better view from here anyway," Casey said.

As they sat there, watching the door, Casey's cell phone rang. He pulled it out, looked at the screen and answered, "Hi, Uncle Jay."

"Where are you guys? I hoped you were going to stay up in your room until I got back."

"You didn't tell us to stay there. Sorry."

"Don't worry, it's not a problem. I just need to take you to the police department. Where are you?"

"We're out in front of the hotel. Wait, why are we going to the police department?"

"They want to talk to you about what you and Johnny overheard. Stay where you are, I'll be down in a couple of minutes."

"Alright."

Casey turned to tell Johnny about the call and noticed that a small gathering of people had surrounded them. Johnny was facing away from Casey, looking at a guy who was sitting on the wall next to him. The guy was facing people on his left, so Casey couldn't see his face.

Casey tapped Johnny's leg to get his attention. "Who's that?"

As he was asking, world renown skateboarder, Kyle Price, turned and said, "Hey Casey, how ya doin'?"

"Oh it's you! I'm good, Kyle, how're you?"

"Excellent. What could be bad? We've got a beautiful day. We're at the Olympics. All is good." Kyle was signing autographs as he spoke. He was surrounded by kids of all ages with hats, helmets, and skateboards in their hands, waiting for his signature.

"Are you here as a spectator? Skateboarding isn't an Olympic sport, is it?"

"No, not yet. I'm doing some exhibitions before the games begin."

"Cool."

"Hey, there's a session this afternoon. Why don't you guys come? You can hang out with me and the guys up on top of the half pipe."

"Wow. Really?" Johnny said.

"Really what?" said Jay as he squeezed through the crowd.

"Kyle invited us to join him at his skateboarding exhibition this afternoon."

"I take it they mean you," Jay said, looking at Kyle. "I'll guess you're Kyle Price."

"Yes, and you are?"

"Jay Scott, Reid Clark's and AllSport's Chief of Security. Nice to meet you."

They shook hands. "Great to meet you, too."

"I need to borrow these two for about an hour."

"Okay, I'll see you guys later, right?" Kyle said.

"You bet," Casey said. "Where's the skate park?"

"Next to the aquatics building. Be there at two and I'll bring you up top. We start at 2:30."

"We'll be there," Johnny said.

"You too, if you want to come, Jay. Casey, why don't you bring your dad?"

"I doubt he can make it. I'm pretty sure he'll be on the golf course."

"Okay, I'll see you later."

"See ya, Kyle," Casey said as he and Johnny followed Jay around a corner to a waiting police cruiser.

Chapter 3

"SO, I WAS told that you two have proven yourselves to be excellent junior detectives," said Chief of Police, Kevin Coyne. Sitting at the boardroom table next to Chief Coyne was Mathew Morrow, the president of the Australian Olympic Committee (AOC).

The boys glanced at each other and smiled. "I guess so," Casey said. "It helps that people aren't intimidated by us like they are by police or investigators. We solved the case at AllSport because we overheard things in the gym that would never have been said if cops were present. We were there preparing for our black belt tests and we kind of stumbled upon the conversation unintentionally."

"Right. And now I'm told you did it again, but this time the situation is much more serious. Mr. Scott tells me that you overheard a discussion between hired killers. Is that correct?"

"Yes sir," Casey said.

The Chief nodded. "I see. Well, boys, I'll admit that if this hadn't been brought to my attention by Mr. Scott, I probably would have considered it just a prank by a couple of teenagers. I wanted to meet you two before I put a big team on this. You seem like good kids. There is no way you'd make this all up, would you?"

"What?" Johnny said loudly. "Are you crazy? Make it up? Why would we do that?"

Johnny was so loud that the four security officers in the adjacent room turned from the wall of video monitors that they were viewing and looked through the glass partition in the wall. The technology in the Olympic Security offices was very elaborate. Joysticks and keyboards allowed the officers to switch between and control a vast array of cameras that were placed strategically at each Olympic venue, inside and out, as well as throughout the streets of the Olympic Village.

"Sir," interrupted Casey. "I promise you, we're not making this up. The conversation we heard this morning was real. A man and a woman are planning to kill or kidnap an Olympic gymnast."

"I'm sorry boys. I didn't mean to offend you, but I'm sure you understand the importance of this situation. A situation like this is severe no matter when or where it occurs. But, at the Olympics it has the potential to become a world crisis. When the press gets wind of this, all hell is going to break loose around here. Uh, sorry for using bad language. I'm not exactly used to working with kids."

"No problem, we've heard worse," Casey said.

"I'll bet. Anyway, after meeting you and hearing it from your mouths, I believe you."

Morrow nodded in agreement.

Chief Coyne looked at Jay. "I'd like your help with this, Jay. These boys may prove vital to catching this couple. I want to make sure that when their parents hear about it, they're okay with it. I think you can help with that, right?"

"I wouldn't have it any other way, Kevin," Jay said. "The boy's fathers already know about it. Johnny's dad is one of my top men and he's one of Casey's dad's bodyguards. They're together now out on the golf course and will remain together until we catch this couple. The boy's mothers, on the other hand, don't know about it yet. They're not going to be very happy when they hear that the kids are involved."

"I'm sure," the Chief said.

"I'll handle it," Jay said. "They'll be alright."

"I'm glad *I* don't have to tell my mom," Johnny said making a face. Casey and the men couldn't keep from laughing.

"You think it's funny? Uncle Jay, you know her. Just be ready to run after you tell her."

Jay chuckled again. "I'm afraid you're right. She's not going to take it very well. I'm going to need your help. And yours too, Casey."

They nodded and looked at each other again with wide eyes and worry on their faces. "Scary thought," Johnny said.

"Yup," Casey agreed.

"Okay guys, if you're ready, I'd like to get down to business," Chief Coyne said. "I want to bring these two down before the Opening Ceremonies. All in all, the Olympic Security force is about 20,000 strong. While we need to keep this situation fairly quiet, I want to start positioning people by later this afternoon. We're currently running background checks on all the guests staying at your hotel and every other hotel in the area. Jay, I'd like to hear any thoughts you have on how to proceed."

"I've got some ideas already," Jay said. "Talk to the boys first and then I'll tell you what's on my mind afterwards."

"Good. Okay boys, I'm all ears. Which one of you wants to start?"

The boys looked at each other and Johnny quickly pointed at Casey.

Casey told the Chief everything that he'd told Jay and the others earlier. When he was finished and Johnny had nothing to add, Chief Coyne drummed his fingertips on his hardwood desk, looked over at Morrow, and said, "Matt, do you have any questions?"

"No, they seem to have covered things very well. I'm impressed boys."

"Thank you sir," Casey said. "But, we're just telling it like we heard it."

"Well, I don't think many kids your age would have remembered all the details like you've just explained them."

Casey and Johnny looked at each other and shrugged.

"Okay, Jay," Chief Coyne said. "Will you tell us your ideas now?"

"Of course." Jay glanced down and spun the trackball on his Blackberry. "First, we need to check with the hotel and see where they have cameras. We'll need to review all of them, especially the elevators. Casey will have to evaluate whichever images may be a match. We may have to install some extra covert cameras depending on where they have them already. We'll need a few on each floor, especially on floors ten through fourteen."

"Why especially those floors?" Morrow asked.

"Because Casey saw the elevator stop at twelve after the guy got in. If these two are professionals, chances are, they never let their guard down. The way they avoid getting caught is that they always suspect and act as if they're being watched. Professionals in their business typically avoid leaving a trail of crumbs that lead to their doorstep. Things like getting off an elevator, either one or two floors below or above their floor, and taking the steps the rest of the way is commonplace among the pros."

"Makes sense," Morrow replied. "Glad you're here, Jay! But let me ask you both, how do we wire so many cameras so quickly?"

"We'll use wireless covert cameras that are hidden in smoke detectors, exit signs and pictures," Chief Coyne said. "They're simple to install."

Jay continued, "We should also put a few in the gym. Chances are, if they exercised one morning, they'll do it again. We also need to get some undercover people working in the hotel. We'll need a few in housekeeping, room service, maintenance, one or two at the front desk. We could also use a few in the bar and in the restaurant." Jay waited for Chief Coyne to stop writing.

"If we don't find them immediately, we'll need to broaden the scope of the investigation. We'll also need to supply protection for all the top female gymnasts."

"That's going to be tough to do without raising suspicion," Chief Coyne said.

"If it gets to that point, raising suspicion won't be a concern anymore," Jay said.

"God, I hope we find them fast," Morrow said. "It'll be a complete disaster if the press gets hold of this."

Jay raised his brow and said, "Mr. Morrow, with all due respect, you should make sure your people are prepared for a press conference, but don't call for it until we tell you to. Finding this couple is going to take some time. Installing the cameras may be fairly easy, but it's time consuming. We'll have to wait long enough for the system to record activity, which will then need to be reviewed. Then, when we find people that fit Casey's sketchy description, he'll have to verify whether it's them or not. The suspects are more likely to make mistakes if they don't know we're on to them. Once word gets out they'll go further undercover. That's when we'll have no choice but to raise the protection level on the gymnasts and all other athletes. At that point this place is going to get pretty stirred up."

"Right mate, like a hornet's nest," Chief Coyne said.

"Kevin, we better inform Desko," said Morrow.

"Who's that?" Jay asked.

"William Desko, he's the commissioner of the AFP," Coyne said.

"AFP?" Casey asked.

"The Australian Federal Police. They're the equivalent of your FBI," Coyne said.

"Wow," Johnny said.

"He puts his pants on the same way you and I do, Johnny, one leg at a time," Coyne said.

"Huh?"

"I think he means that you shouldn't be so impressed. He is just a regular guy," Casey said.

"Exactly!" said Coyne. "He's good, but he's a hothead. If he hears about this from the press he'll blow his cork because we didn't bring him in on it immediately. I'll call him as soon as we're done here."

"Speaking of that, are we almost done?" Morrow asked. "I have a two o'clock meeting with some Olympic officials from Russia."

They all looked at the clock on the wall. It was 1:10.

"Uh oh," Casey said quietly.

"What's wrong?" Jay asked.

"It's no big deal. Johnny and I were supposed to meet our moms for lunch. We were supposed to call them at 12:30. They probably called, but Johnny and I shut off our phones so we wouldn't interrupt the meeting."

"You better call her now."

"Yeah, but what do I tell her? They don't know about all this yet."

"Hmm, right," Jay said. "Let me think." He rubbed his chin and took a moment. "Ok, tell her you're with me. Say that we were offered a tour of the Olympic Security offices and that you were asked to shut your phones off during the tour. At least it's not a total lie. If they want, I'll take you to them as soon as we're done." He looked at the clock again. "Say around two-ish."

"No Uncle Jay, Kyle invited Johnny and I to watch his exhibition from the top of the half-pipe at two o'clock."

"Half-pipe? Kyle? You're not talking about Kyle Price by any chance, are you?" Coyne asked.

Casey nodded.

"Wow! My son would kill to meet him. He practically lives on his skateboard."

"If you can get him there, I'm sure we can get him up on the platform with us."

"Really? That'd be great! Okay, I'll call him while you call your mom. Then we'll finish up and you guys can go. Where should I tell him to meet you?"

"Hmm, that's a good question. I have no idea. Why don't you just give him my cell number, or better yet, explain it all to him and then let Johnny talk to him to give him our cell numbers."

"Okay. Just a warning, he's a bit of a wise guy."

Casey nodded. "Skateboarders are all wise guys."

"Hey!" Johnny said.

"What? Don't tell me you're going to argue? You're the king of wise guys!"

"Who me? Well ... yeah, I guess I am."

They all chuckled.

Chief Coyne and Casey made their calls. After they both hung up, Coyne looked at Jay and said, "You ready to finish your list?"

"Yeah, sure." Jay lifted his Blackberry and said, "Casey mentioned that it sounded like the killers were talking as if the mob had hired them. I'm going to call a mafia boss I know back in the States to see if he can dig up any information."

"Why would a mob boss help you?" Morrow asked.

"It's a long story. Let's just say we've known each other for a long time and he kind of owes me. Plus, he's a big sports fan and he loves AllSport."

Morrow gave a look of confused acceptance.

"How about you, Kevin? Do you have any organized crime contacts you can ask?" Jay asked.

"The only ones that I know are in lockup and they're not too fond of me. It probably has to do with the fact that I put them behind bars. Desko probably has some possibilities. I'll ask him when I call."

"Good." Jay looked down and rolled his Blackberry trackball. "Okay, I think we should put some plainclothes teams out at the gymnastics venues. How many facilities are there?"

"Two practice sites and two competition arenas," Coyne said. "I'll put undercover people in maintenance and housekeeping uniforms at each site. I'll do the same at all the dorms and cafeterias."

"Good. You should also send teams to scout out the areas surrounding each of the facilities. We'll need to post teams at every location within range of a sniper rifle. Rooftops, high-rise offices, and apartments. Anyplace that your people feel has even a remote possibility. Obviously, they should err on the side of caution."

Jay waited again for Coyne to catch up with his notes. "This one's a long shot. You should check with every gun shop and arms dealer you can find. With heightened security at just about every airport in the world, chances are they flew in without weapons, so they would've had to pick them up here. If they were hired by locals, the weapons would probably be delivered or placed somewhere for them to pick up. It'll be easier if they were hired by anyone other than a local, because that way they'd have to buy the guns once they arrived. As I said, it's a long shot and it could all be a waste of time if their plan is to poison or strangle their victim instead of shooting her."

That statement brought a loud groan from Morrow.

They all briefly looked at him.

"Sorry, but this is getting to me."

"There's no need to apologize," Jay said. "You've got a lot on your hands."

"Jay, if you're done, let's adjourn this meeting. Matt's obviously had enough and I have a ton of work to do." He ran his finger down the list in front of him as he said it.

"Alright, I'm done. Can we get a ride? I want to take the boys sneaker shopping, then drop them off at the skateboard event and head back to our hotel to speak with their mothers."

"Sneaker shopping?" Casey complained.

"Oh, you're such an idiot," Johnny said. "He wants you to find sneakers that match the ones you saw the guy wearing so we all know the color and style."

"One for Johnny," Jay said, putting his finger up and making an invisible check mark in the air.

Chief Coyne chuckled and said, "I'll have the same officer who brought you here take you back. In fact, I should probably have him stay with you. You're going to need to get around a lot until we nail these people. You'll be better off with someone who knows the area."

"Thanks. Do you think we can use an unmarked van? I really prefer not to draw any attention to me or the boys and we have a pretty big group traveling with us."

"Of course."

**

A loud, "Oooh," emanated from the massive crowd as skate-boarder, Avi Malina flew high into the air in a rapid spin. But at the peak, his board flew away and he dropped like a rock, slamming hard onto the wood floor of the half-pipe.

"Oh, that had to hurt!" Johnny yelled.

"Yeah, did you see the height he had? His board was about five feet over our heads at the top of his jump," Casey said.

"He's not getting up too quickly either. He had to be almost twenty feet in the air when he lost his board. That's a huge fall."

"Look, he's getting up." Casey yelled as the crowd roared with approval. "What was that trick anyway?"

"It was a kick flip McTwist, mate! I can't believe we just watched that right in front of our eyes," yelled Chief Coyne's son, Dylan.

Casey turned toward him and said, "Pretty cool, huh?"

"Cool? This is unbelievable! I can't thank you enough. You totally rock, mate!"

When they first met him, Casey and Johnny had been shocked. His earrings, tattoos, black, skin-tight clothes and sneakers along with his long, pitch black hair were the antithesis of his straight-laced dad, Chief Coyne. Looking at his rail-thin torso made it hard to believe he could really ride the skateboard in his hands. Dylan was quiet; in fact he had barely said a word before he'd belted out his last statement.

"Are you guys having fun?" Kyle Price asked them as he walked up next to Dylan. He bent over and put his board down at the edge of the pipe.

"Great show so far, Kyle," Johnny yelled. "How is Avi?"

"He'll be okay. 'Fraid he's out for the rest of the exhibition, but at least he didn't break or tear anything … this time."

"Glad to hear it," Casey said.

"And now," blasted the announcer through the obscenely loud sound system. "The reason you're all here. The master of skateboarding, Mr. Kyle Price!"

"Later, boys!" he said as he kicked his board over the edge and dropped into the pipe.

"Somebody pinch me." Dylan's jaw was almost touching his chest. "Am I dreaming, or was Kyle Price really just standing next to me?"

"Yes, Dylan, he was, and you better pay attention to him unless you want to miss it."

"Miss what? Don't tell me he's going to do a 900?"

"Yup. He promised to do it right in front of us. Watch close."

Just as Casey finished saying it, Kyle flew up into the air in front of them and spun two and a half times and landed almost perfectly. The crowd exploded in screams and cheers. Casey looked at Dylan who was hugging his skateboard tightly with his jaw wide open, once again.

After Kyle finished his ride, he grabbed a microphone and made a quick statement, thanking his fans. He turned to the boys and said, "Hey guys, I'm glad you came. I'm going to go sign some autographs and give away some t-shirts. Hopefully I'll see you during the next few days."

"Thanks, Kyle," Johnny said.

"See you later," said Casey. "Hey Kyle, before you go, could you sign Dylan's skateboard for him?"

"Sure, man. Nice to meet you, Dylan." Kyle grabbed the board and signed it.

"Thanks, mate, uh, I mean, Mr. Price," Dylan stammered.

Kyle slid down the pipe and the boys climbed down the stairs, left the skateboard park and started walking toward their hotel.

Chapter 4

"THEY'RE NOT SERIOUS, are they? Grilled kangaroo fillets?" Casey said, wrinkling his nose.

"And what the heck is curried Yabbie?" Johnny asked.

"It's a crayfish," said Charley, the plainclothes officer that Chief Coyne offered to drive Jay and the group around.

"Come on, boys," Casey's dad said. "There's plenty of stuff on the menu that you like."

"Yeah, and if we eat all our kangaroo can we have wattleseed pavlova or baked quince for dessert?" Johnny said.

"I'd rather have an anzac biscuit," Casey said.

"Casey, do you have any idea what anzac stands for before you go making fun of it?" Jay asked.

"No, is it a fruit?"

"Australian New Zealand Army Corps. The biscuits were originally made by the wives of soldiers during World War I to be sent to their husbands in battle."

"Really? That's pretty cool."

"I figured you'd think so."

"Uncle Jay, how do you know so much?" Johnny asked. "You're like a walking encyclopedia."

"Yeah, I'm loaded with useless information, aren't I?"

"Can we order already guys? I'm really hungry," said Casey's dad.

They all ordered and discussed the day. Reid's round of golf with the American team would usually have been the main topic of the evening, but tonight was different.

"So, boys, we heard you had a rather exciting day," said Casey's mom.

The boys glanced at each other.

"Yeah mom, Kyle Price's skateboarding exhibition was awesome!"

"Uh huh, I'm sure it was. But, wasn't there something that happened earlier in the day?"

"Uh, yeah, I guess there was."

"Well?"

"Well, do you want to hear it from the beginning, or do you just want to hear that we'll be careful?"

"Considering Uncle Jay has already told us the whole story, I guess hearing that you'll be careful ... *really, really* careful, will have to be enough."

"We will be, we promise. Right, Johnny?"

"Huh?" Johnny turned to look at Casey. "What did you say?"

"Have you heard anything we were talking about?" Casey asked.

"Yeah, sure."

"Well, tell me?"

"Tell you what?" Johnny asked.

"What were we talking about?"

"Huh?"

The others at the table laughed and shook their heads a little at Johnny's silliness.

"Oh forget it. What got you so distracted? What were you looking at?" Casey turned to look and saw a pretty, blond girl at the far side of the next table looking at them and smiling. He turned back to Johnny. "Oh, now I get it."

The others saw her too. "All right, Johnny! Go get her, tiger," his dad said.

"Dad! Stop!"

Joel Rebah smiled. "C'mon, send her a Shirley Temple or something."

"Leave me alone! She's smiling at Casey now, anyway. They all smile at Casey."

Just then the girl's family stood and as they were preparing to leave, she started walking in the boys' direction.

"Oh, look, here she comes." Joel said. "I'm glad *she's* got some nerve, anyway."

"Dad, stop! She's coming over to meet Casey, you'll see."

The girl walked towards them and stopped next to Casey.

Everyone's smiles at the table weakened a bit. They all knew how popular Casey was and that girls were always attracted to him. For once it would have been nice if Johnny got the girl's attention.

"Hi, Casey, I'm Samantha. It's nice to meet you. I've seen you on TV and magazine covers, like forever." Her Australian accent was heavy.

"Hi Samantha, it's nice to meet you too."

"Would you introduce me to your friend?"

"Sure. Samantha, this is Johnny. Johnny, meet Samantha."

Johnny almost fell as he shot out of his seat and said, "Hi Johnny, I'm Samantha."

A small chuckle emanated from around the table. Johnny's face reddened as he realized his blunder.

Samantha continued as if she didn't hear his mistake. "Hi, Johnny. It's really nice to meet you. I know you boys are probably only here for a little while, but if you want to hang out during the Olympics, it would be fun."

"Uh …" Johnny glanced at Casey who was nodding aggressively while mouthing, *say yes.*

"Sure, that sounds great," Johnny said.

"Good. Here," she said, handing him a napkin. "I have to go now."

"Bye," Johnny said.

"Call me," she said as she turned and walked to the exit with her family. Just as she was walking out the door, she turned again and waved her fingers at Johnny.

Johnny flopped back into his seat looking at the others. Their smiles couldn't have been any bigger.

"What?" Johnny's attempt at nonchalance was ridiculous.

"What, my butt," Casey said.

"Casey! Watch your mouth," said Shane.

"Sorry, Mom." He turned back to face Johnny. "Dude, that was awesome! She's gorgeous. You are so lucky."

Johnny slowly smiled. "Did that really just happen?"

"Yeah, baby. My son was just picked up. I love it," Joel said.

"*Dad!*"

"Honey, cut it out," scolded Cindy. "He's embarrassed enough without you adding to it."

"Embarrassed? Who's embarrassed?" Johnny said.

They all laughed.

"So, what's on the napkin, champ?" Jay asked.

"What napkin?"

"The one in your hand that she just gave you, you idiot," Casey said.

He looked down at the napkin. "Oh," he said, surprised. He opened it, and his eyes grew wide, as did his smile.

"So, what's it say?" his mom asked.

"It's her number."

"Yeah," Casey said, looking down at the napkin. "It's her number with call me and her name all surrounded by a big heart."

"Wow, you got an aggressive one, buddy. Better watch out for her," Reid said.

"Yeah, I hope so!" Johnny said.

The men all laughed and the women rolled their eyes.

"Just like his dad," said Johnny's mom, shaking her head.

"Send her a text," Joel said. "I'll bet she's in the car staring at her phone right now, waiting and hoping."

"Maybe she'll send me one."

"You didn't give her your number, you idiot?" Casey said.

"Casey, stop calling him an idiot, would you please?" Shane said.

"Ma, we call each other idiot all the time. I don't mean it. I only mean it when I put stupid in front of it."

Shane rolled her eyes and sighed. "Whatever."

Johnny had his cell in his hands. "What should I say?"

"How about, hi, it was nice to meet you."

Johnny fumbled with his phone. "I can't type. My hands are shaking."

"Here," Casey said, holding his hand out. "Let me do it."

Johnny looked at him. "Just tell me what you're saying before you send it."

"Don't you trust me?"

"With my *life*, yes, but not with my *girl*."

Everyone laughed out loud at that one.

"That was a great line, Johnny!" Reid said.

"So, you want me to tell her or not?" Casey said with his hand out.

Johnny handed him the phone.

As Casey typed away, Reid Clark said, "Okay folks, it's time for me to hit the hay. Let's go."

Casey handed Johnny his phone as they all walked out and got in the unmarked police van. The boys sat in the far back. Within minutes, Johnny's phone chimed with a message.

"Oh my God," he whispered to Casey. "She answered."

"Well, look at it, you jerk."

Johnny nervously looked at the text and smiled. "She asked if she can come to our hotel tomorrow afternoon with a friend."

"Tell her if her friend is as pretty as her, then yes."

Johnny started typing. "Wait, you really think I should say that?"

"Sure, it is a little obnoxious, but it's also a compliment. *I know*, tell her *I* said it. Then she can't get mad at you."

"Wait, then it'll look like you think she's pretty."

"Well, I do."

"Yeah, I know, but *I* should be telling her that, not you."

Johnny's phone chirped again with another message. He looked at it and laughed quietly.

"What's it say?" whispered Casey.

"She said, what's with the delayed answer? It's Casey right? Tell him not to worry, my friend is really cute."

Casey laughed very loud. "Are we that obvious?"

"I guess so."

"What's so funny back there?" Johnny's mom asked.

"Nothing," Johnny said.

"Sounds pretty funny, for nothing."

The boys just looked at each other and smiled.

"You better answer the message. Ask her what time they're coming and also ask what her friend's name is."

Johnny's thumbs moved like lightning and his smile stretched from ear to ear as he and Samantha sent messages back and forth for the rest of the ride.

**

At the hotel, as they were walking through the lobby, Johnny tapped Casey's shoulder and motioned with his head for Casey to look at a guy he hadn't seen before behind the reception desk.

Casey shrugged, nodded and said, "Maybe?"

Jay was walking behind them and obviously noticed their gestures. He caught up to them and quietly said, "I was thinking the same thing, but it's hard to tell. We haven't been here long enough to know who's a regular and who's not. I wonder if they've installed any of the new cameras yet. Speaking of which, I spoke with Chief Coyne. They downloaded some of the video from the elevators. He wants you at police headquarters tomorrow morning. What time do you want to go?"

"How about nine? Johnny and I need to be back here by twelve."

"What's going on at twelve?" Jay asked.

"Uh, kind of a double date," Johnny said.

"Really? Is that what you guys were laughing about in the van?"

"Yeah," Casey said. "I hope the other girl is as pretty as Johnny's."

"Blind dates can be fun."

Casey gave him a funny look.

"Never heard of a blind date? It's when you have a date with someone you never met."

"Oh."

As they all rode the elevator and walked to their rooms, Johnny, Casey and Jay kept looking up.

"What are you guys looking at?" Reid asked.

Casey dropped back to walk with his dad. "We're trying to figure out if they've installed the new wireless covert cameras yet."

Reid looked up. "I don't see any."

Casey laughed quietly.

"What's so funny?" his dad asked.

"I said covert. You're not *supposed* to see them."

"Alright Mr. Detective, go ahead and laugh at me. I'll show you covert." Reid punched Casey's arm.

"Ow, dad, why did you hit me?"

"That was my covert punch for laughing at me."

"Covert punch?"

"Yeah, you didn't see it coming, did you?" Reid said with a big grin.

"Oh, really funny," Casey said, rolling his eyes and rubbing his arm.

Johnny and Jay were chuckling up front. "Actually, it *was* pretty funny," Johnny said.

"Oh, shut up!"

They were at Casey's parents' door. "Good night," Shane said, swiping her keycard. She turned to give Casey a hug. "What time should we meet for breakfast?"

"We're going down to Police Headquarters to look at the elevator videos. I guess we'll need to leave here at around 8:30, right Uncle Jay?"

"Yes, 8:30 will give us plenty of time."

"So, how about we meet downstairs for breakfast at 7:30?" Shane said.

"Okay, see you then. Good night," Casey said.

"Hey, not so quick, champ. Give me a hug," said Casey's dad. As they hugged, he asked, "How's your arm?"

"It's fine. I was only kidding when I said ow."

"Good. Hey, maybe if you're not so busy on this case you and Mom will come out and walk the golf course with me before the games begin. It's really a beautiful course."

"That sounds great."

"Okay, good night, champ. Have fun tomorrow."

"Thanks Dad, good night."

Everyone else went to their rooms and as Johnny pulled out his keycard, Casey said. "C'mon let's go check out the twelfth floor."

"Really? You want to go now? Can't we just go to sleep and do it tomorrow?"

"You can, if you really want to, but I'm going up. In case you forgot, there's a life at stake here and we're the only ones who might be able to identify the killers."

"Forgot? How can I forget when you keep saying it? C'mon, let's go."

They started walking towards the elevator and Johnny asked, "Have you at least thought about what we're going to do if we see them?"

"Nope."

"Oh, great," Johnny said, shaking his head.

As they got to the elevators, Johnny was about to push the up button when he turned and saw that Casey had continued walking. "Where are you going?" he said too loudly.

Casey turned and put his finger to his lips, "Be quiet! Just come on and follow me." When they reached the stairway entrance, Casey said, "Uncle Jay said that they probably use the stairs a lot for the final few floors. I want to check them out."

Johnny nodded as they walked into the stairwell. "Makes sense, I think. On second thought, what do we do if they walk by us in the stairwell?"

"Just say hi and continue. Remember, they don't know we were there this morning."

"Okay."

They walked quickly up the stairs and through the door to the twelfth floor. Johnny immediately looked up and began studying the red exit sign. "You think they put one in there?"

"I don't know."

Johnny waved at the sign.

"Stop it."

Casey stopped talking as they heard the ding of the elevator. Johnny looked at him with wide eyes. His hands were out, palms up, and he whispered, "What do we do?"

Casey waved for Johnny to follow him and began walking down the hallway toward the elevator. Two couples had gotten off the elevator and were walking toward the boys, talking a little loudly and laughing as they walked. As the boys passed them, Johnny looked down while Casey looked right at them.

"Evenin' mate!" said one of the men.

Casey nodded and quietly said, "Hi," as he and Johnny continued past. As soon as the people were far enough away, Casey turned his head and whispered, "I don't get it."

"Get what?"

"Just follow me," he said as he turned around to follow the people after they turned the corner in the hallway. Casey was now walking quickly.

"What's up?" Johnny said, quickening his pace to keep up.

"Shh." They were now walking as fast as they possibly could, while making sure they couldn't be heard. They slowed down as they reached the end of the hallway and Casey put his back up to the wall near the inside corner. He slowly peered around the edge. He needed to be quick, but not so fast that he'd draw their attention. He didn't want them to see him, yet he needed to see what room they were entering. The hallway was empty. He heard their muffled laughter getting quieter and then he heard their door close.

"Oh man, I missed them."

"Why were you so interested in them? Neither guy had blue running shoes and neither woman had a brown ponytail. In fact, they both had long black hair."

"Yeah, I know. That's why I followed them," he said as he rushed down the hallway trying to listen to each door he passed.

"What are you doing now?"

Casey turned toward Johnny with an irritated look, and mouthed, *shut up*.

Johnny put out his hands in frustration and mouthed back, *what are you doing?*

They reached the end of the hall without hearing any noises from within the doors. The hallway was a dead end. On their way back, they listened to each door, once again. Nothing.

Once they turned the corner, Johnny whispered, "Can I talk yet?"

Casey shook his head and continued walking. When they got back to their room he looked at Johnny and said, "I'm sure one of those women was the one I saw in the hallway downstairs. But, her hair was different and those people had Australian accents. The woman downstairs was blond and said bonjour to me in a French accent."

"Maybe it was her in a disguise," Johnny said. "They're hired assassins; chances are they probably wear all kinds of disguises."

"That's what I was thinking. What time is it? We need to tell Uncle Jay right away."

Johnny walked over and looked at the digital clock on the nightstand between the beds. "It's only ten after ten."

"Good, at least we won't be waking him." Casey grabbed his cell and dialed Jay's number.

"Hello?"

"Uncle Jay, it's me."

"What's up, Casey?"

"Did I wake you?"

"No, I'm watching a movie. What do you need?"

"I think we may have found them."

"Ha! I should have known you two wouldn't just go to sleep. Give me a couple minutes, I'll be right there."

"Okay." Casey hung up and said to Johnny, "He's on his way."

"Do you really think it was them?"

"Why else would someone wear a wig and speak different languages?"

"I don't know, but would assassins hang out and get drunk with other people?"

"I don't think there's a rule book for assassins."

"I guess you're right. I just figured that they'd probably try to keep a low profile."

"I would have thought so too. But, don't forget we're dealing with criminals. Cold-blooded killers. They probably do whatever they want to do, whenever they want to do it."

"It's so weird."

"What is?"

"I can't believe were working on a case trying to catch assassins."

"Yeah, it is kinda weird."

A knock at their door stopped the conversation. Johnny got up and let Jay in. He was wearing jeans, a t-shirt and sneakers.

"So, talk to me," he said. "What ya got?"

"Do you remember the woman that I talked about that had said bonjour to me downstairs after Johnny and I overheard the talk between the assassins?"

"Sure I do."

"I'm pretty sure we just saw her with another woman and two men up on the twelfth floor."

"Pretty sure?"

"The woman downstairs had blond hair and said bonjour with a heavy French accent. The woman on twelve had the same face, but dark hair and they were Australian."

"The hair could have been dyed or a wig. The voice and language is pretty easy to fake with practice. Did her height match the woman with the ponytail?"

"Yes."

"What room are they in?"

"Well, we know which hallway, but not the specific room. They walked by us and we had to let them turn the corner before we followed. When I turned the corner they were already in the room. I heard a door shut, but I didn't see which one. The rooms were 1240 to 1260."

"I wonder if they installed cameras in the hallways yet." He looked at his watch. "Actually, it doesn't matter. It would take too long to view the video anyway." He paused for a moment. "Okay boys, we have a decision to make. We either go in with force or we keep it very low key with undercover officers dressed in hotel maintenance uniforms. If you're sure it's her, we should use force and get this thing over with quickly. But, if you're not absolutely sure, and it turns out not to be them, then using force will probably tip off the real killers, wherever they are, and force them underground."

Jay looked at Casey and waited.

"Wow, Uncle Jay, you want me to decide that? I'm not positive."

"Then the decision is made. I'm going to call Coyne and get a few of his people up here. Hopefully, he's already got a few dressed in maintenance uniforms."

Jay made the call and found that Chief Coyne was actually downstairs in the hotel setting up his undercover team. Jay hung up, looked at the boys and said, "I'm sure you heard that he's here. He's on his way up with some of his men."

"Can I turn on the TV while we wait?" Johnny said as he sat down on the small couch.

"Are you serious? All this crazy stuff is going on and you want to watch TV?" Casey asked.

"I'm just freaking out and I thought it would help."

"Go ahead Johnny," Jay said. "If it'll help, turn it on, but please keep it quiet. I need to think."

"Uncle Jay?" said Johnny as he turned on the TV.

"What?"

"Can I order something from room service?"

"Are you serious? Can't you wait till we're done?"

"You're unbelievable," Casey told Johnny.

"I didn't have any dessert tonight! I didn't think it could hurt to ask."

"Johnny, I'll tell you what," Jay said. "If it's them and we nail these bas ... these people, I'll get room service to bring you as much cake and ice cream as you can eat."

Johnny smiled and snuggled on the couch as he channel surfed. He stopped for a moment on the Yankee game just in time to watch the Phillies end the inning with a double play. The Phillies were up eight to six going into the ninth inning. Johnny changed the channel.

"Hey, c'mon leave the game on," Jay said.

Johnny had already switched the channel to a local rugby game. "Now here's a game. These guys are sick."

"Yeah, you're right," Jay said. "Rugby is great. But, let's watch the last inning of the Yankee game."

Turning the channel, Johnny stopped briefly on a skateboarding show.

"Hey, look, that's from today's exhibition. I wonder if they'll show ... Wow, look, there we are!"

"Cool!" Casey said.

"Holy cow," said Jay. "Was that Kyle Price doing that flipping thing?"

"Yeah, Uncle Jay. That was his signature move. It's called a 900."

"Amazing! Hey, there you guys are again. Who's that guy standing next to you wearing all black? Look at all those tattoos and piercings. He looks a little scary, huh?"

"Yeah, well you better not say that to his dad," Casey said.

"What are you talking about?" Jay asked.

"That guy's father," Casey said, pointing at the TV, "is on his way up here right now."

Jay was silent in thought for a moment. "Wait a minute. You mean that's ... No way!"

"Way!" Johnny said, nodding.

"*That's* Coyne's son?"

"Yup. Hard to believe, huh?" Casey said. "That's what we thought when we met him. He's actually a pretty nice guy."

"I'll bet they have an interesting relationship," Jay said.

"Johnny said the same thing earlier."

"Wow," Jay said, shaking his head. "Johnny, do me a favor. Change back to the Yankee game, would you please?"

"Fine, but baseball is so boring."

"Not when you have something riding on the game," Jay said.

"*You've* got money on the game?" Johnny asked.

"Not exactly. Mort Mann, an old friend of mine, lives down in the Philly area. We have kind of an ongoing rivalry. When the Yanks win, he buys me dinner. I buy when the Phillies win. We have the same deal with the Eagles and Giants."

There was a knock on the door as he said the last few words. Jay walked over and opened it. Chief Coyne and six officers in maintenance uniforms walked in.

Each officer had a bag slung over their shoulder. Jay turned to Chief Coyne. "What's in the bags?"

Coyne nodded to one of his men, "Show him."

The officer reached in his bag and pulled out a canister. "A flashbang," he said as he laid it on the desk next to him. Then he pulled out a Glock, a taser, and handcuffs, naming each as he lined them up on the desk.

Then Chief Coyne said, "Alvarez, go ahead, show him your toys, too."

A female officer stepped toward the desk, reached into her bag, pulled out an interesting looking automatic pistol and laid it next to the other weapons on the desk.

"Whoa!" Johnny said. "I want to shoot that one!"

"I think not," Jay said. "It's an M&P15, right?"

"Yeah, I got a few from Desko today. Smith & Wesson is trying to convince him to arm all his people with them."

"Heck, they could convince me pretty easily."

"Yeah, me too," Coyne said. "Okay, why don't you give us the details so we can get this search underway?"

"We know the hallway they're in, but not the room or rooms. I think this is how we should play it. We should position a team at each end of the hall and one in the middle. Chief Coyne and I will back up teams one and two in the hallway and I'll call one of my guys in to back up team three." Jay turned toward Casey. "Why don't you tell them what the people looked like while I call Joel?"

"Okay," said Casey. "Well, we saw two women and two men. The woman that was the same as the one I saw downstairs was about this tall." He held his hand to about five and a half feet. "She had black hair this time, but it was blond when I saw her this morning. It looked like a wig, but Jay said it could have been dyed. She had a lot of makeup on both times. But, I looked at her hands this time to check her true skin color. She has dark skin."

"Do you mean she's black?" one of the uniformed officers asked.

"No, she's white but dark skinned. Like ..." Casey looked around the room and pointed to one of the officers. "Like him."

They all looked at the officer's skin color and turned back towards Casey.

"Downstairs she said bonjour to me in a French accent. Up here they spoke English with an Australian accent."

"What about the men and the other woman?" the female officer asked.

Casey thought for a moment. "The other woman was really skinny and a little taller and she had black hair. I didn't pay that much attention to her."

"Did they go into the same room?"

"I don't know. They were already in when I turned the corner to look."

"What about the men?" Chief Coyne asked.

A knock at the door interrupted their discussion. Jay walked over and let Joel in.

"Come on in. We're just laying out a plan of attack."

Joel quickly scanned everyone in the room and then looked down at the desk. "M&P15s? I guess attack is the right word."

"Hopefully, we won't need them. Obviously, we'd all prefer this to end up without any fatalities."

Joel nodded.

"Joel, this is Chief Coyne," Jay said. "Chief, Joel Rebah is my top man. He's also Johnny's father and Casey's father's body guard."

"Nice to meet you," Chief Coyne said.

"You, too."

"Joel," Coyne said. "You're going to be backup for officers John Knox and Lorraine Alvarez."

Knox and Alvarez nodded to Joel. He walked to them and shook hands, "It's my pleasure to work with you."

"You too, sir," Alvarez said.

"As long as I'm making intros, Jay, you'll be paired with Fred Snyder and Anne Burns."

They all nodded at one another.

"Okay, folks," Jay said. "Let's finish discussing the plan and get this show on the road. We are looking for various things: people who fit Casey's sketchy description, wigs, hair coloring or other disguises, obviously weapons, and blue running shoes like these but not necessarily this brand." He held up the sneakers that

Casey had picked out in the store, earlier in the day. "I have a feeling that if Casey is right and these are our killers, things will become obvious very quickly. Chances are they won't hesitate to shoot. And remember, these are assassins. When they shoot, they shoot to kill."

The officers all nodded.

"I take it you're all wearing body armor?"

More nods. Chief Coyne reached into the duffel he had carried in and pulled out two Kevlar vests. "Here guys, take these." He handed vests to Jay and Joel, and then reached back into the bag and pulled out two more Glocks. "Here you go."

Jay and Joel each put on the vests, released the clips in their guns and checked for live rounds.

"Alright," Chief Coyne said. "Here's how you should handle it after you knock on the doors. When people answer, say, 'Sorry to bother you so late, but the bathroom in the room below yours has a lot of water leaking in through the ceiling. We need to check your bathroom.' Most people will let you in immediately; some will check you out through the peep hole before they open the door. Some may call the front desk to confirm that you're really hotel maintenance workers. I have undercover officers at the desk who will answer the phone calls and verify the issue."

"My guess is that every guest will let you in until we find our friends," Jay said. "Chances are they'll probably think it's a setup. We'll have to play it by ear. But be ready and don't hesitate to use your weapons. These people are killers and they'd probably prefer to die than get caught. But they also probably won't hesitate to take you out if they can."

"Okay, is everyone ready?" Chief Coyne asked.

Each officer said, "Ready."

Joel and Jay nodded and headed for the door. Before opening it, Jay turned and looked at the group. "You know what? We look a little intimidating as a group. We don't want to scare anyone who might be in the hallway. Joel, you leave first with your group and head to the far end of the hall." He turned to Coyne. "Chief, your group should leave the room about a minute afterwards and go to the middle of the hallway. We'll leave after you and take the close end of the hall. Last thing, if any group walks into trouble, the backup guy in the hallway, meaning, Joel, Kevin, or me, will say 'Hooyah' loudly enough for the others to hear."

Joel smiled.

"Hooyah?" asked one of the officers.

Chief Coyne said, "It's the U.S. Navy shout. Let me guess, you guys were both SEALs, right?"

Jay and Joel nodded.

"Alright, first team, go," Coyne said.

Joel, Alvarez, and Knox left the room. Then a minute later Coyne and his officers left. Then, Casey stood and walked over to Jay.

"Where do you think you're going, young man?" Jay asked.

"I'm going to stand at the corner of the hallway and watch."

"No, you're going to stay here with Johnny." They looked over at Johnny, who was now sleeping on the couch.

"Oh, come on, Uncle Jay, don't make me stay here. I won't get in the way. I just want to watch. I promise I'll stay at the corner of the hallway."

Jay looked at Casey.

"You need me to identify the woman anyway."

"When we find her, I'm pretty sure it will be obvious, if, in fact, they're even our suspects. If I let you do this you need to stay back at the corner. If, by any chance, there's a firefight and it ends up in the hallway, I want you to swear to me that you'll run back here immediately."

"I swear."

"We need to go, Jay," said Officer Burns after a quick glance at her watch.

Jay nodded. "Okay, let's do it." he looked at Casey as he was walking out the door. "C'mon."

When they got to the corner of the hallway on the twelfth floor, they saw the other teams in position and as soon as Jay and his team were at the first door, they gave a nod.

Casey heard the sound of three doors being knocked on. Joel's team's door was opened first but Casey couldn't hear the discussion. When the door that Officer Snyder had knocked on was opened, Casey listened to the quick explanation of the leak. The guests let them in and after about three minutes, Snyder and Burns came out and shook their heads at Jay.

"Okay, next," Jay said.

The other teams were moving on to their second door as well. They each made it through another three rooms when Casey heard Chief Coyne loudly say, "Hooyah!"

Jay's team was in the hallway and ran towards Chief Coyne. Joel's team was in a room and took a minute to rush down the hall to help. Casey found it very difficult to stay put at the corner. He desperately wanted to be part of the action, but he had given Uncle Jay his word. And that was that. He watched as the other teams entered the room with guns drawn. Casey expected to hear gun shots at any moment. After a few minutes he heard the door open and saw the group emerge from the room without the woman and man. *What's going on?* he thought. *No gun shots, no handcuffs?* Fear kicked in and Casey became apprehensive. Obviously, he had been wrong, but how? There had been so many signs. As the officers walked by Casey, they seemed somewhat upset. Jay was the last to reach him. He put his arm over Casey's shoulder and said, "C'mon, let's go."

"What happened?" Casey asked, desperately wanting to know why they all seemed so sad.

"It wasn't them. I'll explain when we get to your room."

Coyne and the others were all waiting for the elevator.

"We're going down to the basement," Chief Coyne said to Jay. "I have to set up the rest of my teams. We should have all the new cameras installed by the morning. I'll see you two in my office at nine, right?"

"We'll be there," Jay said.

Casey was feeling really weird. He had no idea what had happened back in the room and he was feeling guilty for sending all these people on a wild goose chase. The elevator door opened and Coyne and his people boarded and turned to the front. They were all facing Casey with long faces as the doors closed.

As he and Jay walked into the next elevator that stopped at their floor, Casey said, "Can you please tell me what happened? I feel like an idiot for wasting everyone's time and I want to know why everyone looked so sad?"

"You didn't waste anyone's time. We always need to follow every lead. And you had every reason to be suspicious about them. Just wait, I'll explain everything."

They exited the elevator and walked to the room. Johnny was still sleeping on the couch with the TV on.

Casey turned to Jay. "So?"

"When they entered the room the officers immediately saw some wigs on top of the dresser. It turns out the woman lost all her hair from chemotherapy."

"Chemo? That's what they give to people with cancer, right?"

"Exactly."

"What about the languages? She spoke French then English."

"She's French. And like most Europeans, she speaks English very well, but she has a heavy French accent. Are you sure you heard her speak with an Australian accent?"

Casey tilted his head in thought. "No, I'm not sure. I heard Australian accents but it might have been the others."

"Her husband and the other couple they were with are Australian."

Casey hung his head low. "So, not only did I waste everyone's time, I also scared an innocent lady who has cancer."

"It happens, kid. But, no matter what, as I have already told you, it's always better to be safe than sorry. Your suspicions could all have just as easily been right."

"So, what now?"

"Now, you join your friend over there and get some sleep. You heard Chief Coyne. He's expecting us tomorrow morning to review the video from whichever cameras are already installed."

"Alright. Good night, Uncle Jay." Casey was upset and it showed in his voice.

Instead of leaving, Jay sat on the edge of the bed and said, "Come here and sit." He patted the bed.

Casey sat next to him and Jay put his arm over Casey's shoulder. "I know you think you let us down."

Casey nodded.

"Do you have any idea how many times I have had teams much bigger than tonight's team follow my wrong hunches?"

"How many?"

"Tons."

"Really?"

"Yup, in fact, I've had cops and innocent civilians get shot during raids that were based on my incorrect suspicions. The guilt can really get to you, but in this business you have to make a lot of tough decisions and sometimes you screw up. But, on the other hand, if you avoid making the tough calls because you're scared that they may prove wrong, people may die because of it."

"So, what you're saying is, even if I was wrong, it was still better that we did the search."

"Yes, Casey, sometimes gut instinct is all we have and we need to follow it. To be a good investigator, you need to take chances and then you need to be okay with the results, whether they're good or bad."

"If you say so."

"I do. Now, go to bed," Jay said as he stood. "I'll see you in the morning."

"Good night, Uncle Jay."

"Good night, Casey."

Chapter 5

"HEY SAL, IT'S Jay Scott."

"Jay, it's good to hear from you. How are you?"

"Pretty good. How about you?"

"I'm excellent. Couldn't be better. The sun is shining, my espresso is perfect, and the tomatoes in my garden are big, red and beautiful. What more could I want from life?"

Jay could almost see the smile on DiGiacomo's face right through the phone. "Sounds like you've got it all, my friend."

"Yes, I believe I do. Now tell me, what do I owe for the pleasure of this call?"

"I'd like you to check something out for me, Sal."

"Okay, I'm listening."

"I'm in Australia, at the Olympics."

"You lucky dog, you. You know I love the Olympics. One of these days I should go see them. I think I'd go to the winter Olympics, though. They're a little more exciting to me."

"Well, we have some excitement here right now, too. That's why I'm calling. It seems we have a couple of assassins here looking to either kidnap or kill a young female gymnast."

"And you think I can help? How?"

"When this couple, this man and a woman were overheard talking about the job, they mentioned that they were hired to make sure that the boss' niece would get a medal."

"And you're thinking that they meant a mafia boss? You know, Jay, there are other bosses in the world."

"Yes, Sal, I know. Every company has one. But, obviously I'm on the phone with you because I believe this may be mafia related."

"Yeah, and I'm getting used to the fact that when you have a hunch, you're usually right. I'll do a little digging and let you know what I find. Australia, huh? What time is it over there right now?"

"It's almost 11 p.m. Why?"

"No reason, I was just curious. The games begin in a few days, right?"

"Correct."

"Okay, I'll call you tomorrow and let you know what I find out."

"Thanks, Sal."

"Hey, Jay?"

"Yeah?"

"Find these people, these assassins, and teach them a lesson. Nobody should be out there making money by killing kids, especially the world's top athletes. It's just wrong."

"I agree, Sal."

"I know you do, that's why I like you. You got a big heart, and that's important."

"I'll talk to you tomorrow, Sal. Thanks for your help."

"No problem. But, I'll tell you what. I'm still waiting for the time you call me just to say hello."

Jay chuckled. "I'll surprise you one of these days."

"You do that. Okay, my friend, I'll speak to you tomorrow. Ciao."

"Ciao."

Chapter 6

"HE'S GOT STRAIGHT black hair and a pretty big nose," Casey said, staring at the computer monitor in a back room at police headquarters. "I mean, he's keeping his head down to avoid the camera, but his nose sticks out pretty far. It's thin and pointy too. At least from this angle it is."

"Looks kinda like Pinocchio's nose," Johnny added with a chuckle.

"Is this the only view or is there another camera in the elevator?" Casey asked.

"Nope, that's the only one. At least it's a clear picture, though," Chief Coyne said. "You're sure that's him?"

"Well, the timing is right. But since the only thing I saw originally was his sneaker, I can't be positive. You can't see his shoes from this angle and the only time the camera caught them was when he was walking in and they were too blurry to really tell much. The color seems right, though."

"Wait a second," Johnny said, getting out of his seat next to Casey. "Can I sit there for a second? I think I saw something."

"What did you see?" Jay asked.

"Just give me a second," Johnny said, as he sat in front of the computer and grabbed the mouse. He quickly clicked on the pause button and then clicked and slid the button that backed the video images up. He studied the screen, moved the mouse around and clicked and dragged a few times. "There! Watch as he scratches his head. There's something between two of his fingers."

The others watched as Casey re-centered the image and zoomed in until they all saw a small tattoo at the base of his middle finger. The tattoo was small enough to be hidden when his fingers were pressed together or in a fist. As Johnny zoomed closer the digital image took a second to clear up. It was far from clear but showed a triangle with a dark line running through the middle and a gap at the top.

"Hmm," Jay said.

"What is it?" Casey asked.

"Looks like our friend was in Delta Force."

"Wow, like the game?" Johnny asked.

"No, Johnny, like Special Forces. Interesting that he'd have it tattooed on, though. Most DFs keep kind of quiet about it."

"Obviously, we're not dealing with an average guy," Coyne said. "I'd bet Delta Force can bring out the best in someone, as well as the worst."

"Yeah, there are some interesting characters in all the special forces groups. They are the best at what they do, but when they go bad, they can make formidable opponents."

"Wonderful," Chief Coyne said sarcastically.

"At least we know what we're up against and now we know the guy is American," Jay said.

"Yes, that'll help."

"Oh, by the way, I spoke with Sal DiGiacomo, my mob friend. He's a family boss and he's doing some research for us. He's also a big sports fan. He loves the Olympics and was furious that someone is targeting a kid. I'll be speaking with him again later."

Coyne nodded. "Good. Commissioner Desko is checking our organized crime informants over here, too. I also have a team researching the female Olympic gymnasts. I figured maybe we'll get lucky and come up with a questionable father, uncle, or other family member."

"Very good," Jay said.

"Uncle Jay?"

"What Johnny?"

"Please don't get mad, but Casey and I need to get back to the hotel by eleven. Is that okay?"

Jay looked at his watch. "I thought your date was at twelve?"

"It is, but I want to take a shower first."

"No problem. We can leave in a few minutes."

"A date, huh?" Chief Coyne said.

"Yeah," Casey said. "Johnny got picked up by a cute girl last night while we were at dinner."

"Oh, so we have a new stud in town. Nice going, mate," Coyne said to Johnny.

Casey laughed.

Johnny shook his head and said, "Oh man, can we just go?"

Jay chuckled. "Yes, Johnny, let's go," Jay got up from his chair and turned toward Chief Coyne. "I'm going to see what I can find out about that tattoo. I highly doubt there are many guys with the same one. I'm going to check with a friend of mine who may know more about it"

"Very good," Coyne said. "I'm going to check and see what we've found with the gymnasts. Also, now that we're capturing so much video, I'm going to put a few people on full-time watch and review."

"Maybe you can do the video review right at the hotel? It would be easier for the boys if they don't have to come here everyday. I'm sure the hotel will provide an office or even a guest room."

"Why don't you use our room?" Johnny said excitedly. "That would be so cool."

"Actually, the system we installed provides a live feed of all the cameras over the internet. Our reviewers here can save any images that may match to a separate file that Casey can view from anywhere he can get online."

"Anywhere? Does that mean anyone can access it?" Jay said with concern showing on his face.

"No, it's ID and password protected. I'm told it's secure."

"Good," Jay said, nodding. "Okay, I think we'll go. I'll talk to you in a little while."

"Bye Chief," said Johnny.

"See you later boys, have fun on your date."

Chapter 7

"DID YOU HAVE to choose a sport that nearly every little girl in the world tries?" said DiGiacomo on the phone with Jay. "I swear, I think every guy I spoke to has a daughter or a niece that does gymnastics. It's either that or ballet. And a lot of these guys think their kid is the one who's eventually gonna win a gold medal. And once you get them started, they don't shut-up. Back flips and pirouettes and tutus and leotards. Ain't exactly the kinda stuff I'm used to talking about."

"Well, I'm sorry I put you through it, but did you come up with anything for me?"

"Actually, yeah. I got a few possibilities and I'm pretty sure I'll get some more. So far I got two bosses and two soldiers. The soldiers are American and Italian. The bosses are Russian and Chinese. I'll email you their names and whatever information we've got on each of them. I don't know much about them yet, but I was told the Russian guy is ruthless, so you better be careful."

"Coming from you, my friend, that's really saying something."

Sal was silent for a moment.

"Are you there?" Jay asked.

"Yeah, I'm here. I was just thinking about your last statement. Were you knocking me or was that praise?"

"Praise, Sal, praise. I would never ridicule you."

"I hope not, my friend."

"Alright, thanks Sal. I'll call you tomorrow. Ciao."

"Ciao."

Jay hung up and sat back on the couch in his room. Weary from a bad night's sleep, he put his head back and closed his eyes. He needed to think about the various issues that had arisen from the investigation but he was too tired to think. He drifted off only to be woken by a knock on the door.

"Hold on, I'm coming." He shook his head thinking, *between the phone calls and people knocking at my door, it's tough to get any sleep around here.*

He opened the door and Buck Green walked right in and headed for Jay's mini bar. "Hi Buck, please, come on in," Jay said sarcastically.

Buck turned, popped open a can of Diet Coke and drank most of it in a few big gulps. "Ahhhh, man it's hot out there!" He put the can back to his lips and drained it. He spun around again, re-opened the mini-fridge, and as he was grabbing another soda, he said, "So, what you been doing?"

"Trying to get a little sleep. It's a bit difficult to do around here with the phone ringing and guests knocking."

"Oh, sorry. What are you doing napping at three-thirty in the afternoon, anyway? Don't you have some killers to stop?"

"Three-thirty?" Jay looked at his watch. "Guess I did get some sleep. When I got off the phone with DiGiacomo it was one-thirty."

"DiGiacomo? Why were you talking to him? You think this is a mob thing?"

"Well, the boys said it sounded like it might be and you know that I like to cover every angle."

"So, what did Sal say?"

"He came up with four possibilities so far. An American, an Italian, a Russian and a Chinese guy."

"I've heard both the Russian and Chinese mobs tend to be cold-blooded."

"Yeah, it's true. Sal said the Russian guy is known to be ruthless."

"*Sal* said that?"

"Interesting, huh?"

"If Sal says the guy is ruthless, he's got to be *really* bad!"

Jay nodded and said, "Yup. So where have you been? I haven't seen you around at all."

"I've been in meetings. I have a few clients here in the games besides Reid. I set up some meetings with the marketing directors of a few companies. I have offers for two of my clients already. All they need to do now is win medals."

"Is that how it usually works? You get companies on the hook before the games even begin?"

"Not usually, but a lot of medium size companies know that as soon as medals are around the necks of some of the athletes, the bigger companies make exclusive offers very quickly. The medium size companies will sometimes pay more for an endorsement than the bigger ones, but sometimes they don't even get a chance to make an offer afterwards. Once an exclusive deal is signed for some products, that athlete is more or less off the market. Like everything else in the business, it's just a big game."

"You're good, Buck. Guess that's why they call you the 'King of all Agents.'"

Buck shrugged. "Yeah, whatever. So, where is everyone?"

"Shane and Cindy took Casey, Johnny and their dates to Manly Beach to surf."

"Dates? Wow, guess I've missed a lot around here."

Chapter 8

"WAIT A SECOND. *We're* gonna surf in *that?*" Johnny looked past the rocky beach at the huge incoming wave. Dozens of wetsuit clad surfers were floating around hugging their boards, waiting for their wave. The few who had caught this one were flying vertically down the enormous wall of water. "That's sick!"

They all stood there, watching in their rented wetsuits. They were near the rocks in front of a statue of a guy surfing. They all held their rented boards vertically, resting the ends on the ground.

"Ready? Let's do it," Samantha's friend Chelsea said, taking a few steps towards the water.

"Hold on. You're not serious, are you?" Casey said.

Chelsea stopped and turned. "What's the matter?"

"The matter is, if I go in there," Casey nodded at the huge wave coming in. "Chances are I won't come out. At least not alive."

"But you guys said you knew how to surf," Samantha said.

Johnny looked at Casey and shrugged. "Oh, why not? Let's go." He picked up his board and headed for the water.

"Johnny, hold on!" Casey yelled in order to be heard over the crashing surf.

Johnny turned around. "Come on, you wimp. How bad can it be? It'll be fun."

Casey picked up his surfboard, shook his head and said, "Oh, brother. Why do I let him drag me into stuff like this?"

Just as the boys got to the edge of the water, Samantha yelled, "Hey, are you guys nuts? You need to be an expert to surf *those* waves. You'll get destroyed out there. We're going around the bend to surf the smaller waves."

"You mean this was just a joke?" Johnny said.

The girls laughed. Johnny dropped his board and started chasing them. Casey, more relieved than annoyed at the joke, watched and laughed as the girls outran Johnny. A couple of minutes later, after Johnny had given up on his chase, they all laughed at the situation, picked up their surfboards and walked to an area with smaller waves.

"Now, this is more like it," Casey said.

They spent the next two hours paddling around and riding waves that were by no means ankle-busters, but, nor were they as treacherous as the ones around the bend. Chelsea was, by far, the best surfer of the four of them. Her cutbacks were fast and smooth and she threw an awesome slash that kicked out a massive spray up on top of a wave.

Johnny watched her closely and attempted a slash on the next wave, only to skid off his board in a painful rail bang. As he managed to slither back onto his board, the grimace on his face was horrible. With his voice raised an octave, he said, "I'm heading in, guys. I'm done."

They all paddled back to the beach, dried off and got ready for their drive back to the Olympic Village. Shane and Cindy were waiting for them at the snack stand. They returned their rented boards and wetsuits to the surf shop and made their way to the van.

**

"Wow, that was cool," said Chelsea as a Chinese gymnast performed a perfect double layout off the vaulting horse.

"Yes, it was amazing," Samantha said a little sullenly.

"What's wrong?" Johnny asked her.

"Oh, nothing."

"Then, why do you sound so upset?"

"Because watching these girls practice makes me wonder what I've been doing for the past ten years. I mean, I never thought I was going to be an Olympian, but I thought I was pretty good. Watching them makes me feel like I've been wasting my time."

"Oh, come on, I'm sure you're great," Johnny said.

"She is," Chelsea said. "She's fantastic and she knows it. She did really well in the Junior Pacific Alliance Championships."

"Oh, so you're *really* great," Johnny said.

"Well, I'm not *that* good," she said, pointing at a girl practicing on the uneven bars.

"Yeah, well, Barrie is one of the best in the world," Casey said. "She's America's top contender in three events."

Barrie Froehlich then spun hard into a flawless full twisting back layout and nailed her landing perfectly. She gave a quick arm pump and walked off the mat. As she was grabbing a bottle of water, Casey called out to her.

Her face lit up, and she walked over to them.

"Hi guys," she said, reaching over to give Casey and Johnny each a hug. "Sorry, I'm a little sweaty."

"I don't think I've gotten a dry hug from you since we met," Casey said. "Whether you're practicing at AllSport or you're at a competition, you're always drenched."

"Guess it's one of the disadvantages of being friends with a gymnast."

"Ah, you're worth it," Casey said.

"That was a great routine, Barrie," Johnny said.

"Thanks, it's always easier when the whole world isn't watching."

"I'm sure you're going to do great."

"Thanks, I hope so."

"Whoa, who's that?" Casey asked, watching a pretty red-headed girl nail a double back flip on the floor mats.

"That's Stefanya, she's awesome. She'll probably win the gold or silver for Russia in Floor."

"Nice!" Casey said.

"Oh, put your eyes back in your head, will you!" Barrie said.

"What are you talking about?"

"Oh, come on, Casey. You're staring 'cause she's beautiful."

"No, I'm not. I'm staring because she's good."

"Oh, sure! Hey, sorry guys, but I have to go. I'll talk to you later."

"Bye," Casey said.

Samantha was staring at the boys with her jaw wide open. "You guys are friends with her? I can't believe it."

"She's an AllSport athlete, or she was, anyway," Johnny said. "We've known her for years. She's nice and she's really funny."

"Please introduce me if she walks by again. I'd really love to meet her."

"Okay."

"How many other Olympians do you guys know?" Chelsea asked.

"There's a bunch from AllSport," Casey said. "I think there's like seven."

"That's so cool. Can we meet some of them?"

"Uh, I guess so." Casey looked at Johnny and shrugged. "Theo and Annie probably won't mind."

"Yeah, and how about Jonah?" Johnny said. "He'll be okay with it."

Casey nodded. "Oh, I almost forgot Parker."

"Right, he's really cool."

"What do you think about Marco or Julia?" Casey asked.

"Julia maybe, but not Marco, he's such a jerk."

Chelsea's eyes lit up. "You mean Marco DeCappa? I'd love to meet him."

"No, you wouldn't," Johnny said. "He may be good-looking, but he's a total idiot. The other divers at AllSport hate him. In fact, I think everyone does."

"He's not that bad," Casey said. "He's just a little full of himself."

"Are you crazy? He's so mean and he thinks he's so great."

"He is great!"

"Yeah, well, it doesn't make him better than everyone else."

"At diving it does."

"You know what I mean."

"Alright, alright." Casey pulled a map of the Olympic Village from his pocket and unfolded it. "We're near the Velodrome. Maybe Theo's there. Let's go see."

"Yeah, they'll like Theo."

"Who is he?" Samantha asked.

"Theo Khune is a track cyclist. Have you ever seen track racing?"

"I haven't," said Chelsea.

"No, me neither," Samantha said.

"Isn't the BMX circuit next to the Velodrome?" Johnny asked as they started walking.

Casey looked at the map. "Yeah."

"Maybe Jack is there."

"Who?" Chelsea asked.

"Jack Detomaso," Johnny said. "You'll like him. He's a little crazy, but he's a good guy. He rides like a maniac. Did you ever hear the term, no fear?"

"Sure, it's on a lot of t-shirts," Chelsea said.

"Well, that's Jack. He has absolutely no fear."

"Sounds like my kind of guy," Samantha said.

Johnny's head turned toward her quickly with a curious look. She looked at him and smiled, "I'm kidding."

Johnny grinned.

"Talk about no fear," Casey said. "You guys should see Johnny fight."

"Fight?" Samantha asked with a frown.

"Yeah, he has black belts in Karate and Jujitsu."

"Wow, really?" Samantha asked.

"Yeah," Johnny said with a smile. "So does Casey."

"That's so cool," Chelsea said.

They walked out through the automatic sliding glass doors into the bright sunshine. Samantha and Chelsea put on their sunglasses.

"Wait a second, everybody stop," Casey said quietly but abruptly.

"What's wrong?" Samantha asked.

"Johnny, look over there." Casey nodded to the left.

"Where?" Johnny asked.

"Right over there, sitting at that picnic table." Again, Casey shifted his head and eyes toward the table. "She's holding a map or something. He's got a red hat on and he's eating something."

"Is it them?" Johnny asked with excitement.

"Is it who?" Chelsea asked, turning to look.

"Don't look at the same time!" Casey said sharply. "I don't want them to know we're looking."

"Who are they?" Samantha asked.

"Come with me," Casey said, as he started walking toward another group of picnic tables on the other side of the crowded walkway. The Olympic Village was getting more crowded now every day. The mix of colorful clothing and languages from all over the world made everything exciting. While khaki shorts and shirts with Olympic rings seemed to dominate, there were lots of saris, kimonos, and an abundance of assorted Aussie bush hats.

They found an empty table and sat. After a quick glance, Casey realized the crowd was blocking their view of the couple. He quickly stepped on the bench and sat up on the table. Johnny and the girls hopped up too.

"Okay, so who are they and why are we watching them?" Samantha asked.

Johnny looked at Casey, tilted his head and shrugged.

Casey did the same and said, "This is going to sound a little crazy and you have to promise not to tell anyone, okay?"

The girls looked at him and then at each other. Samantha said, "Come on, just tell us."

"You have to promise first," Casey said.

"What? Are we like, five?"

"Just say it."

Samantha looked at Chelsea again and shrugged. "Fine, we promise."

Chelsea nodded and said, "Promise."

Casey looked at them, thinking of what to say.

"Like I said, this is going to sound strange, but we think they're hired killers."

"What?" Chelsea said a little too loudly, with a chuckle.

"Hired killers?" Samantha said with doubt in her voice.

"Look, whether you believe us or not, right now we have to watch them and follow them if they leave." He turned to Johnny. "Call Uncle Jay."

"What should I tell him?"

"Just get him on the phone and I'll talk to him." Casey turned back to the girls. "Jay Scott is the head of my dad's and AllSport's security team. Johnny and I were at police headquarters this morning looking at video from the hotel elevators trying to ID two people we overheard in the gym yesterday. They were talking about killing an Olympic gymnast in order to make sure another gymnast gets a medal. I'll explain more when we get a chance, but right now I need you two to do me a favor."

"What is it?" Samantha asked skeptically.

"Can you go walk by them and see what the woman is reading?"

"Wait, you want us to go look over the shoulder of a ..."

Chelsea cut Samantha off saying, "Come on, Sam, let's just do it."

"Alright, but this is crazy," Samantha said as they got off the table and walked away.

"Uncle Jay, it's Johnny. Hold on, Casey wants to talk to you." Johnny handed Casey the phone.

"Uncle Jay, we think they're here. We're watching them now."

"Where are you?" Jay said calmly.

"Outside the gymnastics pavilion."

"Are you sure it's them?"

"No, but she has a pony tail and a similar build. And he's wearing the blue sneakers."

"Okay, stay on the phone. I'm going to call Chief Coyne on a different line and we'll get an undercover team over to you immediately."

"Okay."

As Casey heard Jay speaking with Chief Coyne, the girls came back. They were both wide-eyed and began speaking simultaneously. Casey covered the bottom of the phone hoping Jay couldn't hear him as he asked them, "What's wrong?"

"It's a picture of the gymnastics building," Samantha said.

"Not just a picture, though," Chelsea added. "It's one of those drawings. Oh, what do you call it? It shows the details of the floors and ..."

"A schematic?" Johnny said.

"Casey," said Jay on the cell phone. "What schematic? Who are you with?"

"Uh … the girls, Uncle Jay."

"Oh no, you didn't."

"Uh, yeah, I did. I had no choice. We were all together when I saw them."

"Alright, what's done is done. Two undercover officers are near you now. Where are you exactly and what are you wearing?"

Casey looked at the others. "One of the girls is wearing a dark blue hat and white shirt, the other has a yellow shirt. Johnny and I are wearing white t-shirts. We're all sitting on top of a picnic table across …"

Chelsea tapped Casey's arm.

"One second, Chelsea," he said, holding up his finger.

She pointed behind Casey.

"Casey," said a deep voice behind him.

He turned and saw two tall men in warm up suits standing behind him. "Oh, hi," he said to them. Then, he said into the phone, "Uncle Jay, they're here."

"Good. Let me speak to one of them."

Casey handed the phone to the closest officer. "Uncle Jay, uh, I mean Mr. Scott would like to speak with you."

The officer took the phone.

Chelsea turned toward Samantha and said, "This is some blind date. I know you said it would be exciting, but this is crazy."

"Sorry guys," Casey said. "We didn't expect this to happen."

"Are you kidding?" Chelsea said. "This is awesome."

Casey, Johnny and Samantha laughed.

The officer handed Casey his phone. "Okay, so where are they?"

"They're sitting at a picnic table right over … wait, oh my God, where did they go? Did you guys see them leave?" he said in a panic to Johnny, Chelsea and Samantha.

"No," Johnny said. "I've been watching them the whole time. I only took my eyes off them a second ago when Chelsea made that joke."

"C'mon, let's go," Casey said, jumping off the table. "They couldn't have gone far."

"It doesn't matter, Casey," one of the officers said. "We'll never find them in this crowd."

"Well, we have to try. She was studying a schematic of the building, so they probably went inside."

"Did they have anything with them? Something like a gun case or a backpack or anything they could hide a weapon in?" the second officer asked.

"I didn't see one," Chelsea said. "But, then again I wasn't looking for that. I just wanted to see what she was studying."

"Alright, let's go in," the first officer said. "We should break up into pairs so we're not so obvious. Girls, you stay together. Casey, you come with me. Johnny, you go with Tom. Girls, if you see them or anything suspicious at all, call me immediately. Put my cell number in your phones now. Boys, you too." He waited till they had their phones ready and gave them his number.

"Uh, sir?" Samantha said a little nervously.

"Yes?"

"Chelsea and I are kind of new at this stuff. What did you mean by suspicious?"

"Oh, I'm sorry. I didn't mean to scare you. I didn't even realize I said it. Why don't we just split into two groups? Boys, you come with me. Girls, you go with Tom."

Everyone nodded. "Go ahead, Tom. We'll be right behind you."

Tom and the girls walked toward the building.

"Officer?" Johnny said.

"Just call me Luke."

"Alright. Can I make a suggestion?"

"Of course."

"While the girls look inside the building, maybe we should do a quick loop around the outside."

"Good idea. Let's go."

As they made their way around the building, the crowds thinned out. There was really nothing of interest for tourists to see back here, just lots of television and radio broadcasting equipment. They approached two security guards posted at a gate in a chain link fence.

"Sorry guys," said one of the guards. "You have to go back. This area is off limits."

Luke pulled his badge wallet from his pocket and flipped it open.

"Oh, sorry officer. Come on through."

"No apology needed. You're just doing your job."

They walked through the gate and as soon as they were out of earshot, Casey said, "Wasn't that a little too easy? They didn't even look at your ID."

Luke already had his phone open. "Yes, it was. Good catch, Casey. I'm calling the chief now to get them to tighten things up."

Before he pressed the send button on his cell, it belted out a tune. He looked at the ID, pressed a button and put the phone to his ear. "Whatcha got?" After he listened for a moment he said, "Okay, we'll be there in a minute. Do you see the guy anywhere?" He listened again. "Okay, you should probably split up and back away from the entrance. We don't want to tip the guy off. If it is her then he's probably watching from a distance. We'll be right there." He snapped the phone shut and said, "Let's go."

The boys had to hustle to keep up with him. He explained the situation as he walked. "The girls needed to use the bathroom and when they went in, a woman in a gray jumpsuit was on a ladder with her head above the dropped ceiling through a removed ceiling tile. They aren't sure if it's her, but she has a ponytail the same color and length as the woman that was at the picnic table."

Johnny started to run. "Come on guys, we have to hurry."

"Slow down, Johnny," Luke said. "We don't know if it's her. If it's not, they may still be out here. I don't want to bring attention to us."

Johnny slowed to a fast walk. "Sorry."

"It's alright."

"Hey, look. Come this way." Casey turned and walked towards two guys in blue jumpsuits smoking cigarettes near a back door to the building. Casey got to the door and saw that it was propped open by broom stick. As he reached for the door handle one of the guys said, "Can't go through there, mate. Gotta go around the front of the building."

Luke pulled his badge out again and showed it to the men.

"Sorry officer, we could get fired if we let you in here. You gotta go through the front."

"Guys, this is police business. We have to go in, *now*."

"Come on, mate! You're gonna get us fired!"

"Here." He handed them each his business card. "Have your boss call me if he gives you a hard time."

They entered and made their way through a storage room to another big metal door. Luke pulled the door slowly and gave a quick look into the hallway. "Come on, it's clear. Tom said they were at the back of the building. It should be this way."

The boys followed Luke down an empty, brightly lit, ceramic-tiled hallway, which fed into another busier hallway. They passed a men's bathroom entrance and saw a women's a little further down the hall. They stopped before they reached it and looked around. Neither Tom nor the girls were anywhere in sight.

"Come on, let's go find the next one," Luke said.

They passed two concession stands.

"Vegemite?" Johnny said. "What's that?"

"It's Australian spread. You put it on toast. Why?" Luke asked.

"Vegemite sandwiches are for sale at that counter."

"Must be a joke for you foreigners. They don't sell it at places like this."

They saw the next lady's room entrance and stopped again. "There's Samantha," Johnny said, pointing.

"Okay, hold up here," said Luke as he scanned the area. "Do you guys see Chelsea or Tom?"

The boys were looking around.

"Yeah, there's Chelsea, over there, near that Olympic Flag on the wall."

"Right. Now, what about Tom?"

"Right behind you, mate," Tom said.

They all flinched and turned around quickly.

"Sorry, I didn't mean to scare you."

"Surprised is a better word," Luke said. "Did she come out yet?"

"No."

"And obviously you haven't seen the guy or you wouldn't be here talking to us."

"Right."

"Hey, guys," Casey said. "Someone is coming out of the women's room."

An older woman with gray hair walked out.

Except for Casey, all the guys turned back toward each other to talk. Casey watched the gray haired woman as she walked to a concession stand. "Could that be her?"

"Who?" said Luke, as he, Tom and Johnny all spun their heads quickly towards the ladies room entrance.

"The gray-haired lady who just walked out. She's the same height and build. She could have just thrown on that dress and a gray wig."

"Where is she?" Tom asked.

"Over there, at the farther concession stand. She's walking away now. See her?"

"Yeah," Tom said. "I do. Come on, Casey, you and I will follow her." He looked at Luke and Johnny. "You guys stay here and keep watching."

Casey almost had to jog just to keep up with Tom's long-legged strides.

"Don't run, Casey."

"I'm just trying to keep up with you."

"Oh, sorry." Tom slowed down.

They walked quickly, staying close to the outside wall, keeping their eyes on the older woman's flowered dress. Not paying attention to anyone near him, Casey's right shoulder bumped hard into someone and then there was a loud crash.

Startled, everyone around stopped what they were doing to look.

"Hey, will ya watch where you're going?"

Totally embarrassed, Casey was turning his head as he said, "I'm really sorry." His eyes widened as he saw a woman with a brown ponytail, wearing a maintenance jumpsuit, bending over to pick up a ladder. He wasn't sure what to do. He turned his head and saw that Tom had sped up, obviously trying not to be seen. All kinds of thoughts were swimming through Casey's head. *Is it her? I don't really even know what she looks like, except from a distance. Is her voice the same one that I heard the other day? Should I talk to her? Should I help her pick up the ladder? I wish I could just run away!*

She stood with the aluminum ladder and looked at Casey. "You okay, kid?"

"Who me?" Casey said, not really intending to speak.

She rolled her eyes. "No, the other kid that walked into me! Yeah, you! You look like you've seen a ghost. Are you hurt?"

"Uh, no. I'm just … I'm just sorry I bumped into you."

"It's alright, just watch where you're going next time."

"Yeah … sure. Of course," Casey stammered.

"You sure you're alright? You seem a little out of it."

"No, I'm okay, just kind of embarrassed."

"Right then, see ya mate." She picked up the ladder and walked away, towards Luke and Johnny.

Casey wasn't sure what to do. He looked over at Luke, who was watching the maintenance woman. Then, he turned to look for Tom, who was nowhere in sight.

"Nice way to get everyone's attention," Samantha said, suddenly at Casey's side with Chelsea.

"Yeah." Chelsea giggled and quietly asked, "You were using reverse psychology right? Now, you don't have to hide from her and you know exactly what she looks and sounds like."

"Yeah, right," Casey said. "Go ahead and tease me. I deserve it after that." He shook his head.

"So, what do we do now?" Samantha asked.

Casey looked down the hall in both directions. "I'm not sure. Luke and Johnny are following the maintenance worker and Tom is following the old lady."

"What old lady?" Chelsea asked.

"The one who came out of the bathroom before the maintenance worker or whoever that was."

"Oh yeah, I saw her. Why is he following her?"

"Because I wasn't sure if it was a disguise. That's who we were following when I bumped into the maintenance woman."

"Oh, so you really didn't plan that?" Chelsea asked.

"Nope."

"Oops."

Casey nodded. "Exactly."

"So, now that you talked to her, do you think she's the one?" Samantha asked.

"I don't know. The woman in the gym sounded American. This one definitely had an Australian accent."

"It's not all that hard to do," Chelsea said with a very good American accent.

"How'd you do that?" Casey asked.

"A lot of practice."

"For what?"

"Our school plays."

"Chelsea plays the lead in almost all our school shows," Samantha said. "She's great."

"That's awesome. I can't act at all."

"Never mind all that," Chelsea said. "We should go back into the bathroom to see if that woman put anything up in the ceiling."

"You mean like a gun?" Samantha asked. "Are you crazy?"

"Well, it's the only way we're going to know if she's one of the assassins or not," Chelsea said.

The girls both looked at Casey with questioning looks. "Well?" Samantha asked.

"You're both right. If there's a gun up there, we have our answer. But, we should probably wait for the police to check it out."

"No way," Chelsea said. "We shouldn't waste any time. We should find out now, while she's in the building."

"Yeah, that *would* help," Casey said. "But *I* can't go in and I can't recommend that you guys do something that *I* can't do."

"And how will we climb up there, anyway?" Samantha said. "*She* had a ladder."

"Let's go in and take a look," Chelsea said. "Maybe we can climb on a garbage can or something. Casey, you need to stay out here on lookout."

"Are you two sure you want to do this?" Casey asked.

"No," Samantha said.

"Come on, Sam," Chelsea said. "You heard what they said. Someone's life is at stake here. A *gymnast*."

Samantha looked at Chelsea. "I know it's the right thing, but I'm scared."

"I am too, but we have to do it."

"Oh, alright already, let's just get it over with." Samantha started walking towards the bathroom.

"Samantha, wait," Chelsea said, hustling to catch up to her friend.

Casey rolled his eyes and walked quickly after them. When he was close enough, he said quietly, "Girls, will you please stop for one second."

They stopped and turned to face him. "I'm going to watch the entrance from over there," he pointed to a wall across the hallway. "Chelsea, I'm going to call your cell now. I want you to answer it and then let me just stay on the line with you. Put the call on speaker and just hold it in your hand. I'll let you know if anyone is coming in. What's your number?"

He entered her number and called. She pushed the speaker button and he said, "Testing, one, two, three," into his phone.

"Okay, it works. Let's go," Samantha said. "I want to get this over with."

Casey watched as the girls walked through the blue, tiled entrance. Less than a minute later, he said into his phone, "Two older women are coming in."

"There you are," said Tom as he walked up next to Casey.

Casey quickly covered the mouthpiece on his phone so the girls didn't have to listen to his conversation with Tom.

"Where is everyone?" Tom asked.

"Luke and Johnny followed the woman wearing the jumpsuit and the girls are in there." He pointed to the bathroom. He put his phone back to his mouth. "Two young girls are coming in."

Tom looked at him curiously. "What's that all about?"

As Casey was about to answer, Samantha and Chelsea came hurrying out of the bathroom and practically ran to Casey and Tom. Both girls' eyes were wide with fear.

"There's a blue canvas bag up there," Samantha blurted out quickly. She put her hands up to her face and fluttered her hands. "Oh my God, I can't believe it."

Chelsea put her hand on Samantha's shoulder. "Calm down, Sam. Take it easy. It's okay."

"What's going on?" Tom asked. "What blue canvas bag and where?"

"Up in the bathroom ceiling where the woman in the jumpsuit was," Chelsea said.

"You girls climbed up and looked?"

Chelsea and Samantha nodded.

"And you were out here as lookout?" he asked Casey.

Casey nodded.

"Oh my God. You kids are crazy. You can't just do that kind of stuff on your own. That's why *we're* here."

Casey and Samantha looked at him and shrugged. Chelsea said, "You can get mad at us later. Right now you should get someone to get that bag down."

Tom looked at her and said. "How big is it?"

"About like this," Samantha held her hands about two feet apart.

"And you left it up there, right?"

"Are you kidding me? I wasn't going to touch it. I don't know how to handle a gun."

"Shhh, quiet," Casey said.

"Okay, sorry," Samantha snapped back at him.

"How did you climb up to the ceiling?" Tom asked. "Can I do it?"

"No," Chelsea said. "She climbed on the garbage and then jumped up to pipes and hoisted herself up."

"Really?" Tom asked incredulously. "Are you a gymnast?"

Samantha nodded.

They all heard a loud metal clink behind them and turned around. The shocked looks on each of their faces almost made Johnny laugh as he walked towards them from a distance. The noise was made by the ladder being carried by the same woman in the jumpsuit. She was heading back into the bathroom.

"What the heck?" Casey mumbled as he stepped back to hide his face from the woman.

As she carried the ladder into the bathroom, Luke and Johnny stepped up next to the others.

"What's she doing?" Tom asked, looking at Luke.

"I don't know," Luke said. "We followed her back to the maintenance room. She went in and a minute later came back out and walked here."

"The girls checked up above the bathroom ceiling before I got back here," Tom said. "They saw a blue canvas bag up there. I was about to go in and check it out."

"You guys climbed up and looked in the ceiling?" Johnny asked in surprise.

Samantha nodded.

"That took nerve. I'm impressed ... I think," Johnny said.

"Well, it *was* daring," Luke said. "But, you shouldn't have done it. You should leave things like that to us."

"We thought we should do it while she was still in the building," Chelsea said. "We figured it would be easier for you to catch her that way."

"I can't argue with that, but ..." Luke stopped as the woman came out of the bathroom. She had the ladder slung over her right shoulder and the blue canvas bag hanging from her left.

"Stay here, kids. Tom, let's go."

Casey watched as they approached the woman. "Look around for the guy," he said.

They all looked up and down the hallway in both directions. They didn't see anyone suspicious.

Casey looked back towards Luke, Tom and the woman. She had put the ladder on the ground and was handing over the canvas bag. After searching its contents and talking to her, the officers walked back to the kids as the woman picked up her ladder and walked away.

Luke was holding his cell phone to his ear as he and Tom joined the kids. They heard Luke say "It's Detective Roman, let me have Chief Coyne please."

Casey looked at Tom. "Nothing, huh?"

"Tools. She was fixing a leaky pipe in the ceiling and left the bag up there by mistake."

"A leaky pipe in a new building? Isn't that a little odd?" Johnny asked.

"She said that she's been fixing a lot of plumbing problems. The plumbing contractor did a lousy job on this place."

"So, I guess we lost them," Casey said as Luke pulled his phone from his ear.

"Yeah, it looks that way."

"So, now what?" Chelsea asked.

"You guys can go. Enjoy yourselves for a bit. We have a team coming to meet us here and we'll keep looking. Casey, Chief Coyne asked that you call him when you get back to your room later. He's going to give you the web address for the video. He wants you to look at more of the hotel images and some from the cameras here as well."

"Wow, that sounds so cool," Chelsea said. "Let's go do it now. We can help, right?" she said, looking at the detectives. "After all, Sam and I were the last ones to see them up close."

"I can't imagine why not, although it's not up to me. Casey, just ask Chief Coyne when you call him. It's his decision."

"Alright, will we see you guys later?"

"Yeah," Luke said. "The chief put us on this case full-time. I'm sure we'll be seeing a lot of each other."

"Okay, great. Good luck."

Chapter 9

THE DEEP BOOMING bass of hip-hop music filled the streets in front of the hotel. A hip-hop dance squad was in the middle of their performance in the center of the plaza. Casey, Johnny, Samantha and Chelsea exited the shuttle bus. As Chelsea stepped off the bottom step, she broke into some hip-hop dance moves. Continuing to dance, she turned to the others and motioned for them to follow her towards the performance. There was just enough room for the four of them up at the front of the cordoned off stage.

A big painted sign behind the stage read: Urban Dance Project & E.P.I.C. Motion. Urban Dance Project had just finished a routine and was leaving the stage to a big round of applause as E.P.I.C. Motion was coming on.

"Woohoo!" Chelsea yelled, just before raising her fingers to her mouth and letting out an ear-piercing whistle. "Wasn't that awesome? They're so amazing!"

The boys looked at her holding their ears. "Yeah, they're great, but no more whistling, okay?" Johnny said.

She looked at him holding her hands up to her ears and yelled, "I can't hear you!"

"Yeah, exactly!" Johnny yelled back.

As E.P.I.C. Motion lined up on stage, a few of the dancers waved at Casey and Johnny.

"You know them?" Chelsea asked.

"Yeah, they're from New York City," Casey said. "They perform a lot at AllSport. They're great dancers and they're really nice. I didn't know they were going to be here. Did you, Johnny?"

"No."

"Do they need any dancers?" Chelsea asked. "I'd love to dance in New York."

"Maybe you should finish high school first," Samantha said.

"Yeah, I guess so."

The DJ stopped the music and E.P.I.C. Motion took their positions. Then all of a sudden, a new tune blasted through the sound system and the stage came to life.

"Oh my God, they're fantastic!" Chelsea yelled.

They stayed until the end of the performance and then went up on stage. One of the boys' friends told them that E.P.I.C. was performing at the Opening Ceremonies.

After they introduced the girls to the dancers and congratulated them, Casey said, "Okay, guys, we need to go look at the video," Casey said.

**

Up in the boys' hotel room, as the four of them gathered around Casey's laptop studying the images, there was a knock at the door. Johnny got up and opened it.

"Man, I swear, mobsters are all crazy," Jay said as he walked in, before he realized that the boys had company. "Oh, sorry guys. I didn't mean to interrupt."

"No problem, Uncle Jay," Casey said. "We're just looking at some of the video. Chief Coyne gave us the website and our password."

"Hi girls, I'm Jay. I heard you're already a big part of our investigation."

The girls giggled.

"This is Chelsea and this is Samantha," Casey said, motioning toward each girl as he said their names.

"It's nice to meet you both."

"You too," they both said.

"So, have you found anything on the video yet?"

"We just started looking," Casey said. "There are so many images. It's going to take a while."

"Are the pictures clear? Let me take a quick look."

Chelsea moved from her chair to let Jay get close to the laptop.

"Here, let me show you what we can do," Casey said, sliding his finger on the mouse pad. He zoomed in on a shot from behind the reception desk in the lobby.

"That's a very clear picture," Jay said.

"That's a weird saying on that orange hat." Chelsea said about the guy in the picture.

"Cuse is short for Syracuse University," Johnny said. "Lax is short for lacrosse."

"And you know what #1 means, right?"

Chelsea rolled her eyes. "Duh!"

"Just checking," Johnny said with a laugh.

"So, Uncle Jay," Casey said. "What were you saying when you walked in? It was something about the mob."

"Yeah, I just got off the phone with Sal DiGiacomo again. He's been doing some research for me about possible connections with mob bosses and Olympic gymnasts."

Casey nodded.

"So far he's dug up two possibilities. One's a boss in Chicago with a bad reputation."

"Don't all mafia bosses have a bad reputation?" Johnny asked.

"I mean within the mafia world. There's kind of a code within the world of organized crime. As long as the families follow the code and don't cross the line, there's no trouble between them. This guy doesn't seem to care about those rules. Sal is even a little surprised he's lasted this long."

"You mean like … dead?" Johnny held up his hand, swiped it across his neck and made an awful face.

Jay nodded.

"Wow, I thought that stuff only happened in the movies," Samantha said.

"Oh, it's real, alright," Jay said. "Anyway, this guy's niece is on the American team and Sal said he wouldn't be surprised if the guy is trying to help her out, so to speak."

"I can't believe someone would do that," Samantha said. "The whole thing just makes me angry!"

"You and me both," Jay said.

"So, you said there were two. Who's the second?" Casey asked.

"An uncle of one of the Chinese gymnasts is a powerful guy. It looks like he may be part of the triad in Hong Kong."

"Triad?"

"The triad is similar to the mafia over in China."

"Oh," Casey said, then looked at Jay with questioning eyes.

"What?" Jay asked.

"If the mafia has their own hit men, why would they hire somebody else to kill someone?"

"Good question. I've been wondering the same thing myself. But if there's one thing you know about me, it's that I follow every lead until I can remove it from my list. Also, I don't know that much about the triad's MO."

"MO?" Chelsea asked. "What's that?"

"Method of operation. It's another way of saying how they usually do things."

"I can't believe this," Samantha said. "I'm sitting in a hotel room trying to find killers on a video and talking about the mafia and their MO. I feel like I'm in the middle of a movie or TV show. My friends are never gonna believe this."

Jay snapped to attention. "Whoa, young lady, hold it right there. This discussion, in fact, everything that you've been involved with today has to be kept secret for now."

"You mean I can't even tell my parents?"

"I think *I* should speak with your parents. Yours too," Jay said, looking at Chelsea.

"Good, because I know I can't tell them. They'd never let me out of my room again."

"Let me ask you both a question. Now that you see what it's like working on this case, do you want to continue?"

"What do you mean?" Chelsea asked.

"Well, I'm sure at times today things seemed very exciting, but I'll bet there were also moments that you were really scared."

Both girls stared at Jay and nodded.

"The fact is, we may be able to use your help, but that's only if you want to do it and if your parents are okay with it."

"Help?" Samantha said. "How?"

"I don't care what it is," Chelsea said. "I'm in. This is totally cool."

Casey and Johnny chuckled.

"I'd like to get you both inside the girl's gymnastics pavilion and maybe the dorms too. Have either of you ever written for a school newspaper or anything like that?"

They both shook their heads. "No," Chelsea said.

"That's okay. One of you can be the writer and the other can take pictures."

"I'll take the pictures," Chelsea said. "I hate writing."

"Good, I'll write," Samantha said.

"Does that mean you want to do it?" Jay asked.

"I would do just about anything to meet all the Olympic gymnasts," Samantha said.

"How much will we get paid?" Chelsea asked.

Everyone looked at her. "Are you kidding?" Johnny asked.

"*Uh, yeah!*" she said, smiling.

"Okay then," Jay said, shaking his head. "Another comedian. Just what we need. Who is picking you girls up today, and at what time?"

"My parents are picking us up at six," Chelsea said.

"Okay, why don't you call them and ask them to come up to the room. I'd rather talk to them up here in private than down in the lobby."

"Uh, Mr. Scott, it might not be a great idea for me to tell them we're hanging out with the boys in their hotel room."

"Hmm, right. I didn't think of that. Okay tell them to come up to the Presidential Suite. Tell them that Casey's dad wants to meet them."

"That'll work! My dad will be really excited to meet Mr. Clark. He *will* be there, right?"

"Yes, he's there now. He's getting a massage and then he was going to relax a little before dinner. Samantha, give me your home number, so I can call your parents later tonight."

"You can call, but there's no way they're going to let me do this."

"After I convince Chelsea's folks, maybe they'll help convince yours."

Jay's cell phone rang. He looked at the screen and said, "Oh good, I've been waiting for this call. It's about the tattoo." He looked at Casey. "I'll see you guys at six in your parent's suite."

Jay answered the phone and walked out the door.

"The tattoo?" Chelsea asked.

"On the video we watched this morning," Casey said. "The guy was in the elevator and we saw a tattoo between his fingers."

"Uh hmm!" Johnny cleared his throat loudly.

Casey looked at Johnny and rolled his eyes. "Uh, correction, it was Johnny who spotted it." He tilted his head at Johnny. "Happy now?"

Johnny smiled and nodded. "Yup."

"Anyway, we zoomed in on the tattoo and Uncle Jay said it was a symbol for Delta Force, a special ops division of the U.S. military. He was really surprised that anyone would have it tattooed on. It's a pretty secret division. He said he knew someone who might know more about it."

"I swear, this all sounds like it should be in a movie," Samantha said.

"And just think, Samantha, you're playing one of the leading roles," Johnny said.

She giggled. "Yeah, that's so cool. I just hope my parents are okay with it."

"Johnny, is your laptop on?" Casey asked.

"Yeah, why?"

"'Cause I want to Google something while you guys keep looking at the videos."

"Go ahead."

"You guys should switch to the cameras over at the gymnastics pavilion for a while. Maybe you can follow them from where we lost them out at the picnic table."

Casey got up and walked over to Johnny's bed. He sat and opened the laptop and waited for the screen to come to life. He opened the browser and hit the Google button at the top of the screen. As soon as the Google home page came up he typed *kidnapping Peru* in the search box and pressed, Enter. He scanned the headings on the first few pages and said, "Oh, Gross!"

"What?" Samantha asked.

"What did you find?" asked Johnny.

"You don't even want to know."

"Tell us," Chelsea said.

"Alright," Casey said, skeptically. "Johnny and I heard the killers mention that they kidnapped a guy in Peru. So I just Googled it and one of the stories listed is about a gang in Peru that killed people for their fat."

"Eww, that's gross!" Samantha said. "I think I'm gonna get sick."

"Told you it was bad."

"Yuck. Why would they do that?" Chelsea asked making a wretched face.

"It says they sold it for use in cosmetics."

"Oh, gross," Chelsea said. "That's so disgusting. I'm never putting makeup on again."

"Me, either," Samantha said.

"It sounds like that scene in *Fight Club* where he steals the bags of fat to make soap," Johnny said.

Casey nodded.

"Do you see anything there about the kidnapping?" Chelsea asked.

"I have to narrow my search. There are over 300,000 results for kidnappings in Peru."

"Try searching; couple kidnaps man in Peru," Chelsea said.

Casey typed. "That's much better. Now there are only 205,000. You guys keep studying the pictures, I'll search this."

"Actually, we better get going. It's almost six," Johnny said. "Chelsea, did you call your parents yet?"

"Uh oh, no, I forgot." She pulled out her cell and dialed. After quickly explaining to her mother that they should come upstairs, she hung up laughing.

"What's so funny?" Casey asked.

"You should have heard my dad when he heard he was coming up to meet your father. He got so excited it made my mom nervous. She thought that he was going to crash the car or have a heart attack. Oh, I hope he doesn't act like an idiot when he comes up."

"What are you so worried about?"

"You don't understand. When my dad gets excited about something he acts like a little kid. It's really embarrassing."

"Okay, let's go see how he does," Casey said.

Chapter 10

GO BACK TO sleep. *Go back to sleep. Please, let me go back to sleep,* Casey thought as he rolled over in bed after checking the time. It was 4:17 a.m. He closed his eyes for one last try, hoping it would be at least six a.m. when he opened them again. A moment later, he opened them shaking his head in disgust. It was no use. He was up for the day. *Here they come,* he thought. The barrage of thoughts that woke him would now consume his head, ricocheting around his brain until he got out of bed and did something productive to channel his thoughts.

A smile crept onto his face as he thought of Chelsea. *She's really cute,* he thought, *and funny and smart, and full of energy and really excited about helping with the investigation, no matter how scary it is. And she's so cute!*

His smile bubbled into a laugh and he covered his mouth so he wouldn't wake Johnny. *Watching Chelsea's dad meet my father was great. He was so tongue-tied nobody could even understand him at first. Chelsea's reaction was even funnier. She had rolled her big, brown eyes, shook her head, and then covered her pretty face with her hands. She was so embarrassed when she looked at me and said, "I told you he would do this."*

Chelsea's parents had taken Jay's discussion about the investigation very well. Of course, at first they were shocked and nervous about their daughter's desire to get involved. But they quickly agreed that if she could help save another girl's life, she should do it. Chelsea's assignment didn't sound all that dangerous anyway, and it would probably look very good on her résumé when she applied to college in a few years. Her parents also agreed to help Jay convince Samantha's parents. "That's going to take a little bit of work," Chelsea's mother had said.

Casey wondered how that phone call had gone. He'd find out later whether or not the girls were going on their assignment. Then, his thoughts shifted to the investigation. He quietly got out of bed, used the bathroom, grabbed his laptop from the table and got back under the covers. The laptop was in sleep mode. *It sleeps better than I do,* he thought as he tapped on the space bar and rubbed his finger on the mouse pad. His browser was still open to the search he had been doing on kidnappings in Peru. He opened another browser window and typed in the first few letters of the video website until the website showed as a selection. He clicked on it and then typed his username and password. As the pictures began to fill the screen, he clicked over to the search page and began scrolling down. The list was way too long, so he tried to refine it. Searches of 'kidnapped in Peru' and 'assassinated in Peru' both came up with over 500,000 results. *No vacations in Peru for me,* he thought. After digging for a few minutes and coming up with nothing, he clicked back over to the video site.

The outdoor cameras were obviously all dark. The gymnastics pavilion and the hotel hallways were empty. The only activity at the reception desk was the overnight clerk turning the pages of a book. A young couple was sitting on a couch in the lobby, kissing. Casey hesitated briefly and then clicked to the next camera. The water in the pool was perfectly still. The weight room in the gym was quiet. The next view made Casey flinch. A chill went down his spine as he saw the man and woman getting off the treadmills.

"Johnny, wake up!"

"Huh," Johnny moaned.

"Get up, get up, they're in the gym!" Casey was up and putting on a t-shirt and shorts.

"What? Who's here?" Johnny rubbed his face hard and looked blankly at Casey.

"Not here. They're down in the gym. Now get up and get dressed while I go wake Uncle Jay. That's of course, unless you want to go back to sleep while we get them."

Johnny rubbed his face again. "No, I'm coming," he mumbled.

"I'll be right back. You better be ready." Casey darted to the door and out into the hallway in his bare feet. He took a quick look down the deserted hall and immediately thought that knocking on Jay's door would be way too loud. He turned back to his door and reached for his keycard. His pockets were empty. *Oh, no,* he thought. *Why does this stuff always happen when I'm in a rush?* He rolled his eyes as he thought of the stupidity of his question. He quietly knocked on the door. "Johnny, open up," he whispered with his mouth as close to the door as he could. After about ten seconds he said it again. Johnny didn't answer. Casey looked up in frustration, both with himself and with Johnny. *How could he go back to sleep?*

He turned and ran to Jay's door and knocked quietly.

"Who's there?" Jay asked through the door a few seconds later.

"It's me, Uncle Jay."

Casey didn't wait for Jay to fully open the door before pushing through.

"Ouch. Hey, easy does it, champ."

"They're down there right now. They're in the gym. We gotta hurry."

"Don't you ever sleep? I thought I was bad." Jay put his gun down and quickly threw on a shirt and shorts. As he was putting on his sneakers he looked over and asked, "No shoes?"

"I ran here as soon as I saw them. I'm fine without them."

Jay tied his sneakers, grabbed his gun and said, "Let's go."

They hurried out the door and down the hallway to the elevator. Casey pushed the button and looked up to see the red digital numbers change as the elevator climbed up to them.

"I guess Johnny's sleeping, huh?"

"Yeah, I woke him but he fell back to sleep."

They heard the elevator ding and both looked up to see the number twelve shining brightly. They looked at each other and both immediately said, "Stairs!"

Halfway down the stairs, Casey really wished he had his sneakers on. Jay was way ahead of him but he just couldn't go any faster. He heard the door open a couple of flights down and his heart sank. He knew he was going to be too late and he hated missing the excitement. After all, it was his first big case.

He finally made it to the twelfth floor landing and took a second to catch his breath. He turned the handle on the heavy metal door very slowly, trying to keep as quiet as possible. In spite of his desire to barge through the door, he knew he had to slowly peek into the hallway to evaluate the situation.

With the door opened just a crack, Casey heard footsteps approaching rapidly. His heart skipped a beat as he thought, *Is it them? Are they being chased by Jay?* Suddenly, the door was pushed open into the stairwell, knocking Casey over. Scared out his mind, he fell back hitting his head really hard against the metal railing. His body slid to the floor in a heap, unconscious.

Chapter 11

AT 6:30 A.M., as they had agreed on the phone last night, Tom Westmoreland, Samantha's father, drove the girls to police headquarters.

"I'm telling you Mr. Westmoreland, they're going to be perfectly safe," Chief Coyne said.

"You've got to understand, Chief, my kids are my life. I couldn't handle it if anything happened to Samantha."

"Look, first they're going to sit through some training here, and then they're going to the Olympic gymnastics pavilion to mingle with the gymnasts. They're going to be wearing press credentials, so no one will have any idea that they're working with us. They'll also have an undercover officer escorting them wherever they go."

"Why them versus using regular undercover officers?"

"Because we feel it's more likely that the gymnasts will open up to girls closer to their own age than they would to adults."

"I guess that makes sense. So, where's the guy who spoke to me last night? Scott something, I think?"

"It was Jay Scott. You know Reid Clark, the golfer?"

"Of course."

"And have you heard of his foundation, AllSport?"

"I think so."

"Well, Mr. Scott is Reid's Director of Security. He oversees all the investigations at AllSport and manages the team that guards Reid."

"So, I guess your implying that Mr. Scott is good."

"The best."

"That's just great, but I don't see how it has anything to do with the safety of my daughter. In fact, what does Mr. Scott have to do with the safety of the Olympic gymnasts?"

"Mr. Scott and I are working this case together, Mr. Westmoreland. Reid Clark's son is the one who originally overheard the assassins discussing this issue. He and his friend, Johnny Rebah, have been helping us out. They seem to have a knack for being at the right place at the right time. That, plus the fact that four American gymnasts trained at AllSport, and the fact that two hired killers are out there planning to bring harm to a *kid* is more than enough reason for Mr. Scott to want to bring these assassins to justice. He's at the hotel now where we believe the assassins are staying."

"Okay Chief. Although I'm still not completely at ease with all this, I'll accept your explanation. I am leaving these girls in your hands." He sighed. "Please, *please* make sure they stay safe."

"You have my word."

"Bye girls." He gave Samantha a hug and left.

"*Oh-my-God!*" Samantha said. "I thought he would never leave."

"He obviously loves you a lot young lady. You're very lucky."

"I know, but everything is such a big deal with my parents."

"Well, this time they're right to be concerned. Although, there is no danger in what you'll be doing today, the overall issue is quite dangerous and the people we're trying to catch are professional killers."

"Great. Now you're getting me scared again."

"Don't be scared. Be cautious."

The girls nodded.

"Come with me," he said.

They followed him to a meeting room on the second floor. Chairs were lined up as if it was a classroom and a woman was sitting at a desk in the front. A chalk board on the wall had six words printed in big bold letters on top in the center.

Who, What, When, Where, Why, How

"Officer Camadeco, meet Samantha Westmoreland and Chelsea Colter."

"Hi, girls."

"Hi, Officer," Chelsea said.

"Please, call me Donna."

"Okay," Samantha said.

"Why don't you take seats and we'll get started. We have some work to do before we can go over and have a little fun."

"Fun?" Samantha asked.

"You bet. I can't wait to meet those girls. I love gymnastics, don't you?"

"Samantha is a gymnast," Chelsea said. "She competed in the Junior Pacific Alliance Championships."

"Wow, that's great, Samantha. What are your specialties?"

"Uneven bars and floor exercise."

"Mine were floor and balance beam. But that was a few years ago."

"Oh, how cool," Samantha said. "Is that why you're on this assignment?"

"That, and since I was the editor for my high school newspaper, I usually get the assignments that require an undercover reporter."

The girls nodded.

"Okay, are you ready?"

"Sure," said Chelsea.

"I think so," Samantha said.

"I made you each a page of things to remember when you're interviewing. Let's just go down the list, okay?"

They both nodded.

"Number one, when you're doing an interview, you need to make it look and sound real, so make sure you take lots of notes as you go. Start with the exact spelling of your interviewee's first and last name. Then ask their age and the city or town that they live in. Ask when they started in gymnastics and when they began competing. Ask what event they specialize in or which they like the best. Ask about competitions that they've done well in. Then, when you feel that they're getting comfortable with you, you can start asking questions about their family and friends. Ask who in their family is involved with their gymnastics life. Who comes to their competitions or practices? Who is the most interested when they win?"

Samantha and Chelsea kept nodding as she spoke.

"Once they become comfortable with you and your questions, chances are they'll begin to talk more. Remember, no matter how mundane, it helps if you show a genuine curiosity about the subject. The more interested you seem, the more they'll talk."

"What's mundane mean?" asked Chelsea.

Camadeco looked up in thought, "It's kinda like boring."

"Okay," Chelsea said.

"How we doing so far? Are you guys with me?"

"Yes ma'am," Samantha said.

"Good. Never ask questions that can be answered by a simple 'yes' or 'no.' For example, don't ask questions beginning with 'do you think' or 'will you be.' Make sure you ask open-ended questions that will get them talking. It will be hard to catch everything they say on paper so I'm going to get you a recorder. Are we good so far?"

The girls nodded.

"Okay, last thing before we get going. Make sure at the end of an interview you always ask if the person has anything to add. Sometimes, you'll get your best information from that one simple question."

Another nod from each.

"Good. Okay, let's do it. Follow me," she said as she turned and walked quickly out the door.

Still sitting there, the girls looked at each other in surprise. They both jumped quickly out of their chairs and bumped into each other as they raced out the door. They were holding back giggles as they caught up with her in the hallway.

"I was wondering how long it was going to take you two to catch up. I just wanted to see how you dealt with surprise. Some interviewees may actually do that, I mean just walk away if you ask them a question that irritates them."

"Why would we irritate them?" Samantha asked.

"You probably won't on this assignment. In some cases, we have to ask tough questions, like sometimes it's about the recent loss of a loved one. Most people get upset with questions like that, some people just get mad. If they get mad, the interview is usually over, but if you're good, that's when it can get really interesting. Let's take today's assignment for example. We're hoping to find an Olympian with questionable family ties, hopefully a mafia connection or something like that. If we, or I should say, *you*, strike gold, you may get an adverse reaction from your interviewee. They may get quiet, they may get loud, or they may get mad and walk away. I just want you to be ready for anything. A reaction like any of those could be exactly what we're looking for."

"So, what do we do if someone gets mad and walks away?"

"Damage repair can be tough. Sometimes apologies work. Sometimes it takes a little more convincing, like maybe you can say, 'Samantha, I'm so sorry. I really didn't mean to offend you. Sometimes my questions do that without me even realizing until it's too late. How about if I make it up to you with a great headline and picture in our paper?'"

"We can do that?" Samantha asked.

"Honey, if it gets them talking, do it! If we have to, we'll print the story in the police gazette. They may be a little disappointed, but by then it's too late for them to argue and at least you'll be living up to your promise."

"Cool!"

They had followed Officer Camadeco to her desk as she talked. She bent down, opened a draw and pulled out a pocket size digital voice recorder. She handed it to Samantha and said, "It's really simple to use, press the red button to record and then again to stop."

"Even Samantha should be able to handle that," Chelsea said.

"Wow," Samantha said, smacking Chelsea's arm lightly with the back of her hand.

"Well, you're not exactly a wizard with technology, are you?"

"Shut up."

"Alright, girls," Camadeco said. "Let's go get Chelsea her camera."

They took the stairs down to the basement and walked over to the equipment room counter. "Girls, this is Denis Vaughan. He's in charge of all the police equipment that we use day-to-day. Denis, meet Samantha and Chelsea."

They all exchanged hellos.

"We need a camera, Denis," Camadeco said. "We're more interested in its look than the pictures it will take. The girls are going to be posing as reporters, so anything you have that looks like a camera that a newspaper photographer would carry will be fine."

"I've got just the one. Be back in a flash." He looked at them waiting with his brow raised. Getting no response, he said, "Flash, like as a camera flashes?" He held out his hands. "No, huh?"

Chelsea and Samantha smiled.

"Denis?"

"Yes, Donna?"

"'Could you just get us the camera, please?'"

"Wow, tough crowd," he said as he turned and disappeared down an aisle between shelves filled with all kinds of equipment.

"He's actually really funny most of the time," Camadeco said.

"He's kinda cute, too. For an old man, I mean," said Chelsea.

"Old man? He's my age, Chelsea. Are you calling me old?"

"No, ma'am," Chelsea said with a grin.

"He is kind of cute, isn't he?"

"Yeah, kind of. Where's he from?" Samantha asked. "That's obviously not an Australian accent."

"Nah, he's Irish. Lot's of people here call him Paddy, but it really makes him mad."

"So, why do they do it?" Samantha asked.

"'Cause it really makes him mad!" Camadeco shrugged. "Cops will be cops."

"Sounds pretty dumb to me," Chelsea said.

"I agree, but please don't tell anyone around here that I said that."

Samantha reached up and pretended to zip her lips together.

Vaughan returned and put a camera on the counter. "Here you go, girls. This should do the trick."

Camadeco signed for the camera and said, "Thanks Denis. Okay, girls, let's get out of here."

They followed Officer Camadeco out to an unmarked police car and she drove them to the Gymnastics Pavilion.

Chapter 12

ALTHOUGH HIS WORDS were a little fuzzy, Casey heard Jay say, "I need the website and a password for the cameras." Then he waited a second and added. "Yeah, he'll be okay, he's a tough kid. He was only unconscious for about a minute, but I feel so guilty. I can't believe I knocked him out."

"I'm okay, Uncle Jay," Casey said quietly.

Still on the phone, Jay turned towards Casey. "I gotta go. Please get the background checks done on everyone on the twelfth floor as fast as you can." He hung up.

"How're you doing?" Jay asked.

"I'm alright. My head hurts a little, but it's not that bad." He reached and felt the back of his head. "Wow!"

"A lump, huh? I checked as I carried you up. At least there was no blood. Do you remember what happened?"

"Yeah, I remember getting nervous when I heard footsteps. I thought it was them. Then the door slammed open and I fell. What did I hit?"

"The metal railing."

"I guess we finally found something that's harder than my head."

Jay laughed. "I'm glad you're joking." He gave Casey a hug. "I was so scared that I really hurt you badly."

"Well, you did knock me out, Uncle Jay."

"Yes, I did. Didn't I?" Jay sighed heavily. "And something tells me I'm never going to live it down."

"I promise I won't bring it up ... too often." Casey smiled.

Jay smiled and gave Casey another hug. "Stay in bed. I'm just going to go sit over there and review the video. I want to see what these clowns look like. We should have a good shot of them now."

"Did you see them in the hallway downstairs?"

"No, they were already in their room by the time I got there, *if* it was even *them*."

"I can't believe we keep losing them."

"They're pros, Casey. They're still alive because running from the law is a way of life for them. They know how to get around without leaving clues or a trail and when they do slip-up they know how to cover their tracks. I've dealt with many people like them. We just have to wait for them to make a mistake."

"They seem to be making a lot of them already. I mean we keep seeing them and getting them on video. We just can't seem to catch them."

"Well, here's the harsh reality, my friend. You and Johnny are the ones who keep spotting them and the problem with that is you guys don't carry weapons, and you're not big enough, nor are you trained to apprehend them."

Casey nodded, then made a face. "Ow."

"Bad headache?"

"Really bad. It hurt just to nod."

"I'm going to go get some ice and make a compress for you."

"You should probably let Johnny know what's going on, too. And while you're there, could you get my sneakers and some socks for me."

Jay looked at his watch. "It's still early. Why don't we let Johnny sleep? I don't want you to move around for a while anyway." He went into the bathroom and came out with a glass of water and walked to Casey. "Here, take these."

"What are they? I hate taking medicine." Casey studied the pills.

"Oh, come on. Do you think that I'm going to drug you? They're just pain relievers."

"What kind? They don't look like the stuff my mom gives me."

"They're generic acetaminophen."

"I think she gives me the other stuff, ibuwhatever."

"Ibuprofen is an anti-inflammatory; it might increase the risk of bleeding. You shouldn't take it for a concussion, those are better," he said, pointing at the pills in Casey's hand.

"I don't get it."

"Just take them."

Casey popped them in his mouth and drank the water. "Thanks."

"Sure." Jay said, as he walked over and picked up the laptop. He brought it to Casey. "Here, I'll be right back. Go ahead and surf the net or review more video, but don't move from that spot. You need to rest. Hitting your head as hard as you did can be very dangerous. I'm still thinking of taking you to the emergency room."

"What? No way. I'm fine!" Casey closed his eyes trying not to show that he was in pain.

"Sure, you are," Jay said sarcastically. "Don't move an inch or we're going to the hospital when I get back."

"Alright, alright. I promise I'll stay in bed," Casey said.

As soon as Jay left the room, Casey logged onto the computer and started to search the internet. He really wanted to find out about the kidnappings and assassinations in Peru.

Chapter 13

"EARLY? THIS ISN'T early, it's seven a.m." said Barrie Froehlich. "At home I'm usually up at five and in the gym by six."

"Do you mean at AllSport?" Samantha asked.

"AllSport? Wait, now I know why you look familiar. I saw you with Casey and Johnny yesterday, right?"

"Yeah."

"They're so nice, aren't they?"

"Yes, very."

"Do you know them well?" Barrie asked.

"No, we just met."

"They're great. I went to school with them at AllSport while I was training there. Were you interviewing them, too?"

"No, we were just hanging out together."

"I wish I had time for things like that."

"What do you mean?" Samantha asked.

"Are you kidding me? The Olympics are like the best and *worst* thing that could ever happen to a kid. I mean, I'm here by choice and I really love what I do, but it's like jail ... well, not really jail, I mean, I am free, but sometimes it's just too ... uh, I can't think of the right word."

"Restrictive?"

"Yeah, restrictive. I have no time for friends. I mean, of course most of my teammates are my friends, but ..."

"Most?" Samantha probed.

"Well, they can't all be good friends, can they? Most are really nice, but some are real jerks."

"Really?"

"Oh yeah, like Caitlin, she's such a b ... oops, I mean witch," Barrie caught herself and made a face. "And Allie, she's so mean. She thinks she's like better than everyone else. Probably, cause she's got a lot of money. A bunch of the girls think her dad is in the mafia. She acts so ... so?"

"Entitled?" Chelsea asked.

"Yeah, that's it."

Samantha wrote a note on her pad.

"Don't interview her, she'll bite your head off and she won't shut up."

Chelsea smiled.

"Guess I should shut up, too. Sometimes I talk way too much."

"No, Barrie, you're doing great," Samantha said. "I'm really enjoying this. In fact, if you can make time later, maybe we can get together and hang out for a while."

"I'd like that, but it'll be tough. Our schedule is really tight. You know, practice, eat, sleep, practice, eat, sleep. Coach would flip if any of us strayed from the schedule."

"She sounds tough."

"He's a guy and he's really nice, but he *is* tough. I mean, he's gotta be, right? This is the Olympics."

"It sure is."

Barrie nodded. "Well, I better get back before the Kopp comes after me."

"*Cop?*" Chelsea asked.

"Our coach. His name is Mike Kopp. It's a joke around here. You know, be careful or the Kopp will get you."

Samantha laughed as she wrote. "I like that."

"We gotta have some fun, right?"

"Yeah, you do. Barrie, do you think Coach Kopp would mind if we come to your dorm later and just hung out for a while? What do you guys do for fun?"

"There's a game area in the dorm. We watch TV, there's a pool table, foosball, ping pong and of course there's an X-box and a Wii."

"Oh cool, I love playing Wii," Chelsea said. "What's your favorite game, gymnastics?"

"Are you kidding? I get enough of that here. I like Super Mario Galaxy and a lot of us play Rock Band together. It's pretty funny."

"That sounds like fun. So, can we come back with you later?"

"Yeah, I'll come find you when I leave. You're gonna be here interviewing other girls, right?"

"Yup, we'll be around for a while."

"K. See ya later."

"See ya Barrie," Chelsea said as Barrie walked away.

Barrie turned her head and waved.

"She's nice," Chelsea said.

"Yeah, she is."

"You did great with her. That was so much better than the last few interviews. It was like perfect, getting us to go back to her dorm with her later."

"It's funny, it just felt like a natural conversation. It was easy."

"Only 'cause you made it easy."

"I think it was more her than me."

"I don't know about that. Whatever. Let's take a look at the list and see who we should talk to next. Or better yet, what's Allie's last name? I think we should go find her."

Chelsea ran her finger down her list, scanning the names. "Here she is, Allison Grecco. She's from Philadelphia and her top event is floor exercise."

"Okay. Before we go look for her I need to go to the bathroom."

"Me, too. Do you see Officer Camadeco anywhere?" Chelsea looked around. "We should probably tell her."

"Nah, she said we should just go wherever we need to and she would keep us in sight."

"That's funny, 'cause I don't see her anywhere."

"I'm sure she's watching us from someplace. Let's go, I really gotta pee. Where's the bathroom?"

"There's one, right over there," Chelsea said, pointing.

They walked through the blue tiled entrance and went into separate stalls.

"You know what ..." Chelsea started to speak but stopped as they heard the door open.

"I really want a cigarette," said a girl's voice in heavy Russian accented English.

"You smoke? Are you crazy?" said another voice with a Canadian accent.

"I know, I know. It's stupid, I wish I don't start, but now I no quit. I try, but it no work."

"God, my coach would kill me if she caught me smoking."

"Me, too. I don't know vat's more dangerous, the cigarettes, or my coach if he catches me, or that Chinese girl."

"Huh?"

"Oh, you don't know, I thought I told you. Xi-wei, a Chinese gymnast threatened us."

"Threatened?"

"Da! She said something like if she not get medal, somebody would be dead."

"That's crazy! Are you sure she wasn't just saying it? You know, like sometimes you say something stupid like, 'If I don't win, I'll die.' You don't really mean it. It's just a saying."

"No, Natalia, my teammate, was very scared when she told us about it. We ask her same thing as you ask. Natalia said it was threat, not just words."

"Has anyone checked into it? Like your coach or someone?"

"Da. But when we ask about it, first the Chinese managers get mad, then when they finally ask Xi-wei about it, she says she not say it."

"That's really weird."

"Da!"

Samantha and Chelsea heard the door close and came out of their stalls looking at each other wide-eyed in total shock. "Oh my God," Chelsea said. "Do you think?"

"I don't know. But we definitely need to check it out."

"We should tell Officer Camadeco."

"No, not yet."

"What? Why not?"

"Because we're starting to get good interviews and I think it's because the girls are comfortable with us. If they see us with an adult, they probably won't open up to us."

"I don't know," Chelsea said. "I think we should tell her about this. It could be big."

"I'll tell you what, let's try to talk to Allie first and then, if we can, Xi-wei."

"What? No way!"

"Chelsea, that's exactly why we're here. If we're not gonna follow up on a lead like this, then we shouldn't even be here."

"Yeah, I agree, but all I'm saying is we should tell her."

"You're right."

"Good, I'm glad you agree."

"Yeah, right after we speak with Allie and Xi-wei, we'll go tell her."

"Oh, I thought … Oh, forget it. Let's just go find them."

Samantha smiled.

Chapter 14

"LOOK WHO I found roaming the hallway," Jay said as he walked into the room with Johnny behind him.

"How's your head?" Johnny asked.

"It hurts, but I'll live."

"Lean forward," Jay said, reaching to place an ice filled towel compress on the pillow behind Casey's head. "Okay, lean back slowly."

Casey moved his head and neck trying to get comfortable.

"Here, let me adjust it. Lean forward again," Jay said.

"No, I'll do it," Casey said, reaching for and adjusting the pillows and the compress. He put his head back again. "Ow, that hurts."

"Give it a moment," Jay said. "You need the ice to reduce the swelling."

"It hurts more with the ice than without it."

"I'm surprised you're even awake to talk about it," Johnny said. "You hit that banister so hard, I figured you were gonna be out cold for a long time. I'm surprised there's no blood. It really scared me."

"Wait, you saw it?" Casey asked.

"Yeah, I've been up reviewing the videos. The staircase camera recorded your entire fall. I came here as soon as I saw it."

"How did you know I'd be here?"

"I saw Uncle Jay carry you and I figured he'd either bring you here, or the hospital or to your parent's room."

Casey and Jay both nodded as Casey was typing on the laptop like a pro. "Wow, here it is, come look."

"What are you looking at?" Jay asked, walking over to him.

"My fall. Ooh, watch my head bounce off the railing! It hurts just to see it."

"Oh, you're right. That looks painful," Jay said.

Casey played the sequence over and over again.

"Okay, I've seen enough." Jay said. "I have to make a few calls and I need to go tell your parents about this. They're not going to be happy."

"Uncle Jay, I should call my mom and tell her myself. She'll probably handle it better if she hears it from me. If you tell her that I was knocked out and she can't see that I'm alright, she'll freak."

"You're right. I'm pretty sure she's going to freak out anyway, but it'll be much better if she hears it from you."

Jay's cell phone rang. He answered it and walked towards the opened sliding glass doors as he listened. He walked out on the balcony, turned and slid the door closed.

"So, I wonder if Samantha and Chelsea are doing their reporter thing now," Casey said.

"Yeah, they are," Johnny said.

"You spoke to them?"

"Samantha texted me."

"How's it going?"

"I don't know. I only heard from her when they were on their way over to the Gymnastics place. They're with an undercover cop. A woman."

"Good."

The sliding doors opened and Jay walked back in. "That was my friend Eric. We ran a lot of missions together in the SEALs. He's now a general in charge of U.S. Central Command in the Pentagon. He did a little digging into our tattoo issue. Turns out, there was a rogue group of Delta Force guys who banded together after their time in the service. They made a bunch of money as subcontractors. The Pentagon thinks they were responsible for taking out some high level foreign leaders. They all have the same tattoo on the same finger. Of the five he had info on, two are dead. The other three have pretty much vanished. He's going to call me as soon as he has any more information."

"Did he give you their names?" Johnny asked.

"Only their given names. The ones they used when they served. But those names are useless now. Anybody in their line of work has changed identities many times over. Chances are they've had some plastic surgery to help change their appearance, too."

"But what about their fingerprints and social security numbers?"

"These guys made lots of money and used it and their government connections to wipe the slate clean of their original identities. Fingerprints are only traceable if they're in the system. I have their original names, but I'm sure they're basically worthless."

"What are they?" Casey asked.

Jay looked at his BlackBerry and rolled the trackball. "Gerald Butler, Sean Thompson and Steven McAlister."

Casey typed the names onto a notepad on the laptop.

"What are you going to do?"

"When I Google kidnapping or murders in Peru I get so many hits, I just want to see if using any of these reduces the amount of results I get."

Jay laughed.

Casey shrugged. "That's funny? I thought it was a good idea."

"No, it's not funny at all. I'm laughing because I pay some of my people an awful lot of money to come up with ideas that aren't nearly as good as some of the things you come up with. You're good at this. Really good. If you were older, I'd probably make you an offer to work with me full time."

Casey smiled.

"Uh, hmm," Johnny cleared his throat loudly.

They looked at him and Jay added, "You too, Johnny."

"How much?" Casey asked.

"How much what? How much would I offer?"

"Yeah."

Jay chuckled again. "We'll discuss it when you're done with college. Your parents are going to be annoyed enough with me already for knocking you out. I'm not going to have you start telling them I'm offering you a job, too. They'd kill me."

"Are you kidding me? My dad would love it. He'd think it's great that I got a job."

"Maybe a job at a store or caddying or something, not a job solving crimes."

"You know my dad. He'd love it. He loves getting involved with your cases. He was so psyched when Johnny and I solved the trophy case."

"Yeah, well, I guarantee your mom won't share the same enthusiasm."

"Duh!"

"I'm just saying."

"It would be the same with my parents," Johnny said. "Dad would love it; Mom would be totally pissed off."

"I believe that's an understatement! *Your* mother would *really* kill me!" Jay said.

Jay's cell rang again. He looked at the caller ID and answered, "Jay Scott." He listened. The boys were talking to each other until they heard the tone of Jay's voice as he said, "Really?" He listened more. "Do you have someone checking her meds?" Jay walked to the desk and picked up a pen as he listened. He bent down and wrote a note on a room service menu as he listened again. "No, I want to go check her room. Do you know where her roommate and coach are?" The boys watched him and glanced at each other curiously. "What's the address of the dorm?" He wrote more as he listened. "Okay, thanks for the call. I'll call you with whatever I find. Bye." Jay hung up and turned toward the boys.

"One of the top Czech gymnasts is in the hospital. She's a diabetic. She became violently ill after giving herself an insulin injection. It could be just a coincidence or someone may have tampered with her meds. Chief Coyne is heading to the hospital and I'm going over to her dorm. I'll see you in a little while."

Casey swung his feet off the bed. "We're coming with you."

"No, you're not. You need to stay in bed. Johnny, I'm leaving him in your hands. He needs rest. Make sure he stays put."

"C'mon Uncle Jay," Casey said. "That's not fair. You wouldn't even be on this case if we hadn't overheard that original conversation. You can't make us stay here while you do all the exciting stuff. We won't get in the way. I promise."

"Casey, it's got nothing to do with you getting in the way. I already told you, you guys are a big help. But you need to rest. You probably have a slight concussion and too much movement can aggravate it. Your parents are going to be upset enough already. They'd be furious if I dragged you around with a head injury. They know a lot about TBI from your dad's football days. Rest is mandatory!"

"TBI?" Johnny asked.

"Traumatic brain injury. My dad got hit hard when he played college football. TBI is what caused him to stop playing football and start playing competitive golf."

"Wow, I never knew that. So, in his case, TBI was a good thing."

"I guess so. Kind of," Casey said.

"So, I can count on you both to stay here?" Jay said.

"Okay, okay. We'll stay. But please call us when you figure out what's going on."

"Don't worry, I will. And you call me if your head starts to hurt worse, or if you get dizzy or your vision gets blurry or anything like that. I want to hear about it, immediately," Jay said as he grabbed his wallet and got ready to go.

"Johnny, make sure he keeps that ice compress on his head for at least an hour."

"You got it, Uncle Jay."

Chapter 15

"XI-WEI?" SAMANTHA said to a small group of Asian gymnasts sitting on the floor just outside the entrance to one of the gymnasiums.

"No," a gymnast said, pointing at the entrance. "In."

Another gymnast said, "On bars." She held one hand high and the other low.

The other girls giggled.

"Oh, uneven bars?" Samantha asked, holding her hands the same way.

The girls nodded.

"Thank you."

Chelsea and Samantha walked into the gym and looked around. They saw the uneven bars on the far side of the room where a small group was gathered. As the girls made their way over, a woman with a French accent said, "Excuse me, girls, this gym is off limits to the public."

"We're reporters ma'am," Chelsea said. "We're doing a story for the local paper. Care to give us a quote?"

"What's the story about?"

"What it takes to become an Olympic gymnastics champion," Chelsea said.

"Hm, I like that. Come here, I'll give you a quote."

Samantha glanced at Chelsea and smiled as they walked over to the woman.

"Hi ma'am. I'm Samantha Westmoreland." Samantha reached out and shook her hand.

"I'm Yvette Morel. I'm one of the assistant coaches from France."

"Could you please spell your name?"

After spelling her name, Morel said, "So, what would you like me to say?"

"Whatever you'd like."

The girls spent the next few minutes listening, recording and taking pictures of the woman. They really wanted to get over to Xi-wei, but Samantha decided it was better to let this woman ramble on and have her as a friend.

When they finally made it over to the uneven bars, the group had thinned out. There were now three Asian girls near the chalk box, watching another girl on the bars.

Samantha, quietly enough so as not to bother the girl on the bars, said, "Xi-wei?" Two of the girls watching, turned and looked at her.

"Are any of you Xi-wei?"

One put her finger to her lips, "Sh."

The other pointed at the girl on the bars. "That is her."

Samantha and Chelsea watched in awe as Xi-wei performed an amazing series of spins, twists and finally a flawless double back layout dismount. Samantha waited until Xi-wei walked over to her teammates and another girl grabbed the low bar and began to swing. Once the girl on the bars had the attention of the others, Samantha said, "Xi-wei?"

Xi-wei turned, looked at her and said, "Yes?"

"That was a beautiful routine."

"Thank you." Her English was good.

"We're with the local newspaper. Would you mind if we ask you a few questions?"

"Okay."

"Can we go someplace quieter?"

"No, I need to practice. Here is good."

"Okay, no problem. I must say that your routine on the uneven bars was excellent. Is that your best event?"

"No, floor exercise is my best. That is where I'll win the gold."

"You seem very sure of that."

Xi-wei laughed. "I am sure. I have worked very hard for many years to become the best and now I am proud of it. I will win the gold. You'll see."

"Well, considering how great you were on the uneven bars, if your best event is floor, I can't wait to see your routine there."

Samantha tried to keep her next few questions simple. She also tried to continuously praise Xi-wei. She wanted her to be at ease when she asked about her family. Xi-wei answered questions about her teammates and coaches and about her dedication and seemingly endless hours of practice. Things were going very smoothly, Xi-wei was even laughing at a few of her own answers. Then things changed abruptly as soon as Samantha asked, "Your parents must be so proud of you and your accomplishments."

Xi-wei's smile vanished immediately. "My parents are gone."

Samantha looked at her, but didn't know how to react or what to say next.

"They were killed in a car crash when I was ten. I have lived with my aunt and uncle since then."

"I'm so sorry," Samantha said.

Xi-wei nodded and shrugged. "My parents pushed me very hard when I was young. They wanted me to become a champion. I will win the gold for them. I want to make them proud."

"I'm sure they would be with what you have accomplished already."

"No. That's not enough. I must win a gold medal. My uncle says that is all that's acceptable."

"Your uncle?"

"Yes, my father's brother. He and my aunt raised me and kept my gymnastics training the same as it was before my parents died. I wanted to quit when they died, but my uncle wouldn't allow it. He pushed me to continue. He said I owed it to my parents and he owed it to my father to make sure that I didn't quit. He and my father were very close. We lived next door to each other. They worked together. They spent all their time together."

"They worked together? What did they do?"

"Why do you ask?"

"No reason. You said they worked together, I was just curious."

"They owned a construction company."

"What did they build?"

"I don't know. They never talked about it."

"Okay, let's talk more about you."

Xi-wei nodded. "Yes."

Samantha asked more questions about other events and medals that Xi-wei expected to win. She wanted to ask more about her family, but first she had to get Xi-wei comfortable again. Finally, she asked, "Are your aunt and uncle here?"

"Yes, of course. They manage my career."

"I guess there's lots of money and endorsements involved?"

"Yes, and when I win more medals there'll be even more, but believe it or not, I don't really care about it all. I want to win for my parents, not for the money. My uncle wants the money."

"Do you think at some point I could interview him?"

"No! He'll *never* talk to a reporter. He avoids reporters and photographers whenever they come near me. He's *very* private."

"Why?" Samantha asked.

Instead of answering the question, Xi-wei changed the subject. "Do you want to get some pictures of me doing my floor routine?"

"Sure," Chelsea said.

"Let's go."

They followed her to the spring floor in the center of the gym and Chelsea snapped shots as Xi-wei performed an incredible routine. Almost everyone in the gym stopped what they were doing to watch. Samantha watched, but also looked around the room to see the reactions from other gymnasts. She noticed many looks of awe and thought some girls looked a little jealous too. Many pairs of muscular, chalk dusted arms were crossed tightly throughout the gym. As a gymnast herself she understood the feeling. Jealousy, concern and maybe even a little temporary hatred was common in the world of high level competitive gymnastics.

When Xi-wei completed her routine, applause came from the spectators and families of gymnasts in the bleachers and from a few of the gymnasts around the room. Most of the gymnasts however, just resumed practicing on whatever apparatus they had previously been working on.

Samantha and Chelsea congratulated Xi-wei on her powerful program, thanked her for her interview and walked out of the gym.

"We should go talk to Officer Camadeco now," Chelsea said. "We've got to tell her about Xi-wei's threat and her uncle."

"Her uncle?"

"Yeah, don't you think there was something fishy about him?"

Samantha nodded. "You're right. Let's go talk to her and let's get something to eat. I'm so hungry. Did you eat any breakfast this morning?"

"No, we needed to be at the police station so early. I wasn't hungry at all then."

"Same with me."

"Okay, let's go find her," Chelsea said.

"Let's just walk outside. I'm sure she'll follow us out."

Chapter 16

WITH GLOVED HANDS, Jay had gone through pretty much everything in Ivana Vesely's room. He found no signs of forced entry or any other tampering. He was, however, concerned with the contents of a small, zippered, blue vinyl pouch of medicine. He pulled out one of the many bottles of clear liquid and looked at the label. It was an ordinary bottle of insulin. He put it on the table next to him and pulled out another similar bottle. A closer look in the bag revealed many bottles and a bundle of syringes wrapped by a rubber band. As he looked away, something made him look again. A couple of the bottles had different colored metal caps on them. They were blue while all the others were silver. He looked at the label on one of the blue-capped bottles. It was hand-written in what was probably Czechoslovakian, and while Jay knew many things, he didn't know Czech, nor did he know much about prescription drugs.

He pulled out his cell and dialed.

"Chief Coyne."

"Hey Chief, it's Jay. How's the girl?"

"She'll be okay. It looks like she injected too much insulin and it caused hypoglycemia. She was shaking and in a cold sweat when her roommate walked into the room. The roommate called an ambulance and sat with her. Her speech was slurred so badly the roommate couldn't understand that she was asking for orange juice or soda."

"Right, anything with a high level of sugar would have helped."

"By the time the ambulance got to her, her heart was racing and she was having a violent seizure. They gave her a glucose injection and brought her here. They said she's lucky she didn't go into a coma."

"Hey, did the medics by any chance pick up the bottle of insulin that she had just used? I looked around and can't find it anywhere."

"I don't know. Why?"

"Because I looked through her medical kit. There's a bunch of insulin and syringes, and there are also a couple of bottles of different meds. I don't know if they're insulin or something else. The label is handwritten in Czechoslovakian, I think. I'll bring one in for testing. In the meantime, why don't you ask the medics if they grabbed the vial that she just used?"

"The medics are gone already. Hold on, I'll ask the nurses if the medics gave them a vial."

Jay heard him ask the nurses and then get back on the phone. "Yeah, they brought the used vial. I've got it right here. You're right about the label, it's handwritten, probably in Czech. I'll get it translated and tested immediately."

"Is the metal cap on top blue?"

"Yes, Why?"

"Because, all the insulin bottles in her kit have silver tops. The other two vials have blue tops. Maybe it means something, maybe not."

"What do you think it could mean?"

"Well, maybe whoever is paying the killers also paid this girl's doctor to change her meds. You had said she's one of Czechoslovakia's best gymnasts right?"

"Yes, they told me she was expected to win a medal in floor exercise."

"One less top contender in the competition makes it that much easier for someone else to win a medal."

"Good point."

Jay looked at the vial in his hand. "Hey, there's no date on the label of the bottle I'm holding, how about yours?"

"No. Not on the label, just an expiration date on the glass. You really think her doctor took a bribe and gave her bad meds?"

"I know it's a long shot. I'm just speculating. I do it a lot during investigations. Most of the time it's completely worthless, but every once in a while I come up with something good."

"Well, I'll get this bottle tested immediately."

"Good. Let me know what you find. I have to get back to the hotel and check on Casey. I'll talk to you in a little while."

"What do you mean, check on Casey? Is he alright?"

"He's okay. He got knocked out for a little while early this morning. I'm pretty sure he has a slight concussion. He's lying down with an ice compress and pain killers."

"How was he knocked out?"

"Uh, I kinda pushed a staircase exit door a little hard and he happened to be in the way."

"Oooh, that's not good."

"No, not at all."

"Okay, I'll catch up with you later, mate. Please let me know how Casey is."

"I will, and please call me when you know more about the meds."

"You got it."

Chapter 17

"HEY, JOHNNY, COME here," Casey said.

Johnny had gone back to their room earlier to get his laptop as well as Casey's cell phone and clothes. Watching Casey on Jay's laptop had been driving him crazy. Now, he was right in the middle of playing a computer game. "Hold on a second," he said.

"No, come here now. You gotta see this."

"See what?"

"Come here, I'll show you."

Johnny's hands flew rapidly across his keyboard, trying to fin-ish the next level of the game. He put the laptop on the couch next to him and walked over to Casey.

"What's so important?"

"Read this!" Casey said, turning the computer towards Johnny.

Johnny read the short news piece and said, "Yeah, so? It's about a murder in Peru. You said yourself that there must be mil-lions of them. It's like the drug capital of the world, right? You think it's connected somehow?"

"Look at the guy's name."

"Jerry McAllister. So what, it says nothing about a woman and it's about a murder, not a kidnapping. I thought we were looking for a kidnapping by a man and a woman."

"C'mon, this stuff is never that easy. We have to dig and stretch our thinking. Uncle Jay and your dad don't just look at what's obvious, do they? They always talk about digging further. Looking for clues where others won't. That's what we have to do if we're gonna solve this case."

"Okay, but I don't see whatever it is that got your attention, so why don't you just tell me."

"Fine," Casey said, shaking his head. "Look at these." He pointed to the names that Jay had confirmed were rogue Delta Force guys. "Do you see it?"

"Wait," Johnny said. "Go back to the other page."

Casey clicked back.

"Jerry McAllister?" Johnny said curiously, tilting his head. "You mean he mixed his name with one of the other guys?"

"Either that, or maybe he's the third guy, Sean Thompson, and he took Butler's first name and McAlister's last name."

"Sounds kind of stupid. I mean if you're going to change your name to hide, why give any possible clues?"

"Good point, but then we're dealing with assassins, right?"

"Yeah."

"Well, maybe they're smart, but there also has to be something really weird in their heads. They kill people for money!"

"Yeah, that *is* weird," Johnny said. "Okay, so now that we think that this may be the same guy, what do we look for next?"

Casey bit his lip, deep in thought and just looked at Johnny. Then, instead of answering, he just typed.

"What are you looking for?"

"I don't know, I'm brainstorming!"

"What?"

"That's what Uncle Jay calls it when his team sits around and just throws out ideas about a case. I'm just doing it with Google. C'mon, get on your laptop and give it a try. Think of all the stuff we've come up with so far and search for more information."

"Alright." Johnny walked over and plunked himself down on the couch and looked at the screen on his laptop. After a minute he said, "Where should I start?"

"Think, Johnny!"

"Hey, don't get mad. I've never done this before."

"What? You've never Googled stuff? Yeah, you have."

"You know what I mean!"

"Just make believe it's homework research. What would you type if you were looking for ..." Casey looked up in the air thinking. "A Mixed Martial Arts fighter who died in the ring?"

"Nobody has ever died during an MMA fight, have they?"

Casey shook his head. "I don't know, you idiot. I'm just giving you an example."

"Okay, okay. I got it." Johnny said, typing. He clicked a few keys and said, "Nope."

Casey looked up, "Nope, what?"

"No one has died in the ring. Not yet, anyway."

Casey shook his head again and continued his search.

"Give me some ideas of what to search for," Johnny said. "Like those names, what are they again?"

Casey sighed. "Okay, I'll tell you what; let's do what Uncle Jay and the team do. Tell me any clues we have so far and any thoughts you have on the case. We'll make a list and then start searching everything on it. I'll start with Peru kidnapping."

"Or murder!" Johnny added.

"Right," Casey said as he typed.

"Finger tattoos of the Delta Force symbol," Johnny said.

"Good, and there's the mafia possibilities."

"Right, and the gymnast that Uncle Jay is checking out right now. The Czech." Johnny laughed after saying it.

"What are you laughing at?"

"He's checking out the Czech. That's pretty funny."

"She's in the hospital. You really shouldn't be laughing," Casey said.

Johnny looked at Casey with a questioning look. "You're kidding, right? You know I'm not laughing at that."

"Yeah, I know, I just don't feel like joking around."

"Sorry," Johnny said.

"Forget it. It's no big deal. What else can you think of?"

Johnny looked out through the sliding glass doors and tapped the arm of the couch. "How about the money that the guy has on his head?"

"Huh?"

"You know the bounty or whatever they called it. The woman had joked about it, saying that she might even kill *him* if the reward was high enough."

"Oh yeah! She said there was three million on his head. Oh my God. I can't believe I had forgotten all about that."

"Yeah, me too. Until just now, anyway."

"Let's both Google it. Just enter random stuff."

They both went to work. Short bursts of typing followed by long bouts of scrolling on their mouse pads and scanning the screen. They each read, scrolled, typed and scrolled some more.

"Wow, twenty five million," Casey said.

"You found him already?"

"No, that's the amount this terrorist has on his head. One of Osama bin Laden's guys."

"That's so much money, we should go get him," Johnny said.

Casey laughed. "Yeah, right. Here's an article that says the average price for a hit is two grand." He continued to read. "Sometimes it goes up to ten thousand. Wait, those are pesos ...

No, no they're not, they're dollars. It looks like Columbian drug lords pay for hits pretty often. Here's an interview with a few guys that were paid hit men for the Medellin cartel."

"Drug lords? Do you think our guy has drug cartels after him?"

"I can't tell yet. But I'll bet, if those two were hired to kidnap or murder someone in Peru, it probably had to do with drugs one way or another."

Johnny raised his brow. "I hope we don't run into people like that. Drug lords are scary."

"Oh? When have you met a drug lord?"

"I haven't, but you know what they're like in the movies."

"Yeah, I guess so. Alright, let's keep searching."

Again they both stared intensely at their screens as their hands flew across their keyboards.

"I see a few stories where former Delta Force guys actually helped rescue children who were kidnapped," Casey said.

"There's also a bunch of stuff about a Delta Force movie. Oh wait!" said Johnny. "Here's one. Listen to this. It's called, *Escaped.* It says, '*The couple, believed to be Americans, fled from police during a raid of their hideout in Chilca, a small town south of Lima. The police apprehended the couple's kidnapping victim who will remain unnamed at this time as he is believed to be a family member of a well known drug lord.*'"

"Does it say anything more about the kidnappers?"

"I'm looking." Johnny said as he skimmed down the page. "Yeah, here's more. It says, '*Police in Lima received an anonymous tip that the couple, who go by the name McAllister,*'" Johnny stopped reading and spun his head towards Casey.

"Oh my God," they said in unison.

"Keep reading," Casey said.

Johnny continued, "'*The couple, who go by the name McAllister, are known assassins and seem to be working both sides of a cartel war. They were paid by one cartel to murder the unnamed victim, but instead of murdering him*'" *they decided to kidnap him and try to collect ransom from the other cartel. While it takes warped minds to kill for money, especially a cartel member, you would have to be completely insane to contract with one cartel and threaten another at the same time. This couple may be crafty enough to have slipped through the hands of the police, but there's no way they're going to be able to hide from both cartels. On the other hand, our source tells us, the man was a US Delta Force special ops commando. If anyone knows how to hide in plain sight, it would be him. As for the woman, we have no information about her at all, which, in a strange way, says a lot about her ability to hide.'"*

"Wow," Casey said.

"Yeah, we better call Uncle Jay."

"Not yet," Casey said, reaching for the room phone. He picked up the handset, pressed some buttons, put the phone to his ear and waited.

"Hotel operator, may I help you?"

"Yes, could you please put me through to the McAllister's room?"

"Just a second, sir. I'll look them up."

"Okay."

"I'm sorry, sir. We have no one by the name McAllister staying with us."

"Oh, I just met them earlier in the lobby and they asked me to call. I could have sworn they said McAllister. Are there guests with a similar name staying here?"

"Uh, we've got the McCalls. Could that be them?"

"Yes, McCall, that sounds right. Thank you."

"Shall I put you through to their room?"

"Which room are they in?"

"I'm sorry, sir. I can't give out that information. Would you like me to connect you?"

"No thanks, not right now."

"Is there anything else I can do for you?"

"No, thank you," Casey said and hung up. He turned to Johnny and said, "There's a couple named McCall staying here. It could be them."

"Yeah, I heard you on the phone."

Casey picked up his cell and called Jay.

"Jay Scott."

"Uncle Jay, I think we figured out who they are."

"Really? Okay, I'm just parking the van around the corner. I'll be right up."

Casey hung up after Jay did. He then started typing more searches into Google.

"Why did you hang up?" Johnny asked.

"He was just parking. He'll be up in a minute."

"Good. 'Cause I found more stuff. There's a whole bunch of most wanted lists online. I searched on one and found Sean Thompson on the list. It shows a bunch of aliases, including Gerald Butler, Steven McAlister, and different combinations and spellings of each. It also includes Jerry McCall."

"Is there a picture?"

"Four of 'em. One military picture, another with long dark hair, a beard and a moustache, another one that looks really different than the first two, like maybe he had plastic surgery. And then there's another one that says, Computer Age Enhanced Photograph."

Casey swung his feet off the bed and stood a little too quickly. His eyes rolled as the room spun. Luckily, he fell backwards, landing on the bed. But even the soft mattress hurt as the back of his head bounced off it.

Johnny sprang up from the couch to help. "You okay?"

"No, that hurt."

"Can you move? You should put your head back up on the pillow before Uncle Jay gets here."

Casey slowly turned himself around until he had his head resting on the pillow. "It's wet from the melted ice."

Johnny reached across the bed for another pillow and then helped Casey lift himself up to exchange it. As Casey put his head back, Johnny took the wet compress and said, "I'm gonna go fill this with fresh ice. I'll be right back."

"Hand me your laptop before you go."

Johnny nodded, walked over, picked up his laptop and brought it to Casey.

"I'll be right back."

Casey nodded his head very slightly.

Johnny opened the door to leave, and Jay was standing there with his keycard out, obviously just ready to insert it into its slot.

"Hi Uncle Jay, I'm just heading to the ice machine to refill his compress. I'll be right back." Johnny walked past Jay and down the hall as Jay entered the room.

"How're you feeling, champ? Has the lump gone down at all?" Jay asked as he reached behind Casey's head and gently felt the bump.

"I'm alright," Casey lied.

"Oh, is that why you winced when you moved your head forward?"

"It hurts."

"I'm sure it does. Is it like a dull ache or the worst headache you've ever had?"

"Uh, I guess more like a dull ache. It was better before, but I kinda fell back onto the bed and hit it again."

"You what?"

"Don't get mad. I stayed in bed the whole time you were gone, then when Johnny found pictures of the guy on a most wanted list, I got up to go see them."

"Pictures? Where are they?"

"Right here on Johnny's laptop. I haven't seen them yet, either."

Casey put the computer on his lap and angled it so they could both look. He tapped the mousepad and the dark screen came to life, revealing the four pictures.

"Well, would you look at that! So, tell me what you guys have figured out."

"We both searched the internet using combinations of the names you gave us along with murders and kidnappings in Peru. We found an article about a couple named McAllister, who took a job from one cartel to kill a family member of another drug lord. Then instead of killing him, they kidnapped him. Here, why don't you just read the story." He reached for the keyboard and clicked on one of the links at the bottom of the screen.

Jay scanned the story and chuckled. "Wow, these two are nuts. Nobody in their right mind would go up against a cartel, no less *two* of them. Casey, my friend, it seems you and Johnny are going to crack this case yet."

"Yeah, I only hope we do it before someone gets hurt."

"Yeah, that's the goal," Jay said as he took out his phone and rolled the track ball. He pushed send and put the phone to his ear.

"Yeah, Chief, it's me. It looks like the boys hit pay dirt again." He listened. "Oh, sorry, it's just a saying. The boys found pictures on a most wanted list of one of the guys whose name I got earlier. We need to compare the names with the hotel guest list."

"Uncle Jay," Casey tried to interrupt.

Jay held up a finger asking Casey to give him a second to finish.

Casey rolled his eyes and said, "No, wait a second."

Jay shot Casey an annoyed look. "What? Please just give me a second."

"I spoke to the hotel switchboard already," Casey blurted out.

Jay did a double take. "Oh you did, huh? *And?*" He held his cell phone out so Chief Coyne could hear Casey's answer.

"There's a couple staying here named McCall," Casey said. "It could be them. The switchboard wouldn't give me the room number though."

Jay spoke into the phone again. "Did you hear him, Kevin?" Jay listened. "Right, you need to find out what room the McCalls are in. While you're at it, I'm going to have Casey email you the other names. We might as well check them all against the hotel list. Try all combinations of first and last names. I highly doubt it, but the McCalls may be just an innocent couple. It's a common enough name, but I'm just not a big believer in coincidences. Let's get a team up here to check the room. We can use the hotel maintenance ruse again. I don't want to spook them if they happen to be walking down the hall to their room and approach us just as we're going in." He listened again. "Good. Hey, how's the Czech girl?" He nodded as he listened. "Okay. Any word from Samantha or Chelsea?"

Casey perked up at the mention of the girl's names. He waited impatiently as Jay listened to Coyne's answer. While Jay was listening, Johnny returned and helped Casey put the compress behind his head.

"Okay," Jay said into his phone. "Have your guy call me or just come up after he speaks with the hotel manager."

A knock on the door surprised all three of them.

"Go see who it is," Casey said to Johnny.

Johnny walked to the door and opened it a little.

Casey cringed when he heard his mother's voice. He knew she was going to be upset about his head. She was also going to insist that they go to the hospital.

"Where's Casey?" she asked from the hallway.

"In here," Johnny answered.

"Why are you bothering Jay? You should be outside at the pool or at one of the Olympic venues. It's the investigation, isn't it? You're both consumed with it. Casey?" she said through the door a little louder.

"Yeah, Mom."

"Would you come to the door, please?"

"Mom, why don't you just come in?"

Shane Clark walked in and Johnny shut the door.

"What happened, why are you on Jay's bed?"

Jay finished his call and hung up.

"We had a little accident, Shane," Jay said.

"Accident? What's the matter?"

"I hit my head, but don't worry. I'm okay. Really, I am."

"Where did you hit it? Let me see."

"The back of my head."

"Sit up a little. Let me feel it." She reached behind his head and felt the lump.

"Well, at least you were smart enough to ice it. The bump doesn't feel that big. Do you have a headache?"

"Yeah, but not so bad. Uncle Jay gave me some pain relievers so it's getting better."

"How did it happen?"

"I fell and hit a banister."

"It was my fault," Jay piped in. "I pushed open a door and didn't realize Casey was right behind it."

"It wasn't your fault. You had no idea I was there."

"Well, as long as there's no blood and you weren't unconscious. Ice, pain relievers and rest should be enough."

Casey was biting his lip. Johnny had already walked away to the other side of the room.

"Shane," Jay said. "He actually was knocked out for a little while."

"*What? For how long?*"

"Only about two minutes."

"Only two minutes, huh?" Irritation flared in Shane's voice.

Casey was surprised that she was staying so calm.

"Why didn't you come get me?" she said to Jay. "He needs to go to the hospital."

"No mom, I don't. Not now."

"Shane, I'm sorry," Jay said. "I let the circumstances get in the way. I evaluated him and I figured he was better off here as long as he didn't move. I have no excuse for not telling you immediately."

"I'm okay!" Casey said. "Really, I feel good."

"Casey, you don't understand, I almost lost your dad when he was knocked out."

"You mean when he was shot?" Casey asked.

"Yes, it wasn't the bullet hit that worried us. It was his head. He'd already had a traumatic ..."

"I know, Ma. I know all about his TBI. It's not the same with me. I didn't hit my head *that* hard."

"Oh really? Okay, Dr. Clark, I'm happy you can diagnose yourself."

"Come on Mom, don't get like that. Can't we just go to the doctor later? I feel fine. I would tell you if there was a problem."

"Why later? Why not now? It's something to do with this investigation, right?" she asked.

"Yes," Casey said. "We think we figured out who the killers are. If we're right, we will be saving someone's life."

"This is so unfair. We should be taking you for an MRI, but how can I argue with that?"

"That's exactly how I felt," Jay said. "But, again, I apologize. It wasn't a decision I should have made. I obviously should have told you right away."

"Yes, you're right. But, let's move on. What's happening now that's so important?"

"Casey and Johnny may have found the identity of one of the assassins. Chief Coyne has one of his people talking with the hotel manager now to see what room they're staying in."

"Okay, then what?"

"Then we're going in, either to arrest them, if they're there, or search the room if they're not."

"Okay. So tell me what Casey and Johnny are doing during this ... this ... this raid?"

"Mom, we figured all this out. It's only fair if we're there when they get arrested."

"Fair, huh? I don't think so. Casey, this is now police business. These are ruthless killers you're dealing with. They're not going to let themselves get captured without a fight. Sorry, but one family member getting shot is way more than enough for me."

"C'mon Ma, we won't go into the room. Johnny and I will wait in the hallway. We deserve to see this."

"Casey, how do you know that one of them won't come running out into the hallway shooting at everyone in sight?"

"They ..."

"Stop," Shane said, holding the palm of her hand up towards Casey. "Don't even answer that. This discussion is over. You and Johnny are going to stick with Cindy and me this afternoon. We'll head over to the diving venue and then maybe go out for lunch. I had told Marco that we'd come see him practice. It'll be fun."

"Oh, Mom."

"Where is my mom, anyway?" Johnny asked.

"She's down in the spa getting a manicure and pedicure."

"Gross!" Johnny said, with his face scrunched up.

"Does your dad know that you were knocked out?" Shane asked, looking at Casey.

"No, why?"

"Just checking. I'm sure if he knew about it, *he* would have told me immediately."

"Shane," Jay piped in. "I am really sorry I didn't tell you. I can't apologize enough. It was just plain bad judgment on my part."

Shane was clearly annoyed, but her expression showed more disappointment than anything else. "I know ..." She began to say, but was cut off by a loud knock on the door.

"Hold on, I'll be right there," Jay yelled. He looked at Shane and said, "Go ahead, continue."

"Forget it, Jay. Go ahead and get the door."

"Are you sure?" Jay asked her.

"Yes, I'll get over it."

Jay shrugged, walked to the door, opened it and let two men in. They were both wearing gray pants and dark blue sport coats with the hotel logo sewn on the breast pockets. He spoke quietly with them for a few seconds and then turned to Casey, Shane and Johnny. "These are Officers Carnahan and Floyd."

After quick hellos between all of them, Casey said, "So, what's the plan?"

Officer Floyd said, "We have a team coming up in a few minutes including two officers in maintenance uniforms. We have teams in various hotel uniforms at all the entrances, in the stairwells, and in the lobby and basement near the elevators. We have another team heading to the roof and sharpshooters are finding positions on adjacent buildings as we speak."

"Sharpshooters? Okay boys, it's time for us to go," Shane said.

"Mom, no way. This is finally getting exciting. You gotta let us stick around to see it."

"Sorry, Casey, but this is all way too dangerous. These men are trained and paid to deal with things like this. You boys are not. End of story. Now let's go."

"Jay, please talk to her," Casey pleaded.

"I'm afraid she's right," Jay said. "I've already made one bad judgment call today."

"It's just not fair!" Casey said.

"Look, boys," Jay said. "You have both been a tremendous help with this case. Obviously, if it weren't for you guys, we wouldn't have known anything about it, until it was too late. Because of you and all your research, we're going to arrest two assassins before they get the chance to kill a young gymnast. That alone should make you both feel very good. I think at the end of this there may be a couple of honorary junior detective badges being awarded."

"Really? Cool!" Johnny said.

Casey rolled his eyes. "Yeah, whatever."

There was another knock at the door.

"Okay, let's go boys," Shane said.

As Johnny, Casey and Shane left the room, a team of officers entered. Casey noticed canvas bags slung over the shoulders of the officers wearing the maintenance uniforms. He briefly turned his head, looked at the other plainclothes officers and noticed bulges under some of their sport coats and on closer look at the ankles of others. He then noticed that one officer was carrying a much larger and longer black canvas bag. Casey glanced at Jay and shook his head in disappointment.

Jay shrugged and nodded, letting Casey know that he understood.

Casey turned with his head still shaking and walked out the door.

Chapter 18

"IS THAT REALLY all you're gonna eat for lunch? No wonder you stay so thin," Samantha said to Barrie on line in her dorm's dining room.

"It's funny you ask. It used to bother me. But now, I hardly even think about it anymore. I eat mostly protein, veggies and lots of fruit. Once in a while I'll eat some carbs, depending on my energy level, you know?"

Samantha nodded as she picked up a bowl of macaroni and cheese, looked at it and put it back. After studying the assortment of foods, she picked up a plate of yogurt, granola and fruit.

"Don't feel like you have to watch what you eat for my sake," Barrie said.

"I'm not. I eat this all the time."

Chelsea had a cup of yogurt sitting on her tray next to a foil-wrapped cheeseburger and a container of fries. She looked over at Barrie and Samantha, who were looking at her with grins. "What? Protein, veggies and dairy. It's a perfectly balanced meal."

They all giggled.

As they passed the pizza section, Barrie said, "Of course I also eat pizza when we bring it in. We all splurge on pizza once a week."

"Is your coach okay with that?" Chelsea asked.

"Yeah. He's the one who usually brings it in. I'm pretty sure he thinks that if he let's us eat it occasionally, we won't always feel like we're missing out."

"Smart."

Barrie nodded and said, "Do you guys have what you want? Should we go sit?"

"Yeah, I'm all set," Samantha said.

"Me too," said Chelsea.

They followed Barrie out to the dining area.

"Hey Barrie, come sit with me," said a guy sitting by himself at a big round table.

"Hi, Tony," Barrie said. "I have some friends with me."

"There's plenty of room. Sit."

Barrie looked at the girls who both shrugged. "Fine with me," Samantha said.

As they sat down, Barrie introduced them all to Tony Vallone. Tony had a drink in one hand and a book in the other. His arm and chest muscles bulged through his tight Olympic t-shirt. He nodded and said, "Hi," as he put his book down, and then slurped the last of his drink through a straw.

"Tony is the best in the world on the rings," Barrie said, pulling the foil cover off her cup of yogurt.

"We'll see about that soon enough, won't we?" Tony said.

"Oh, don't be so humble," Barrie said in between licks of the foil top. "You can gloat a little when you're the best."

"If I win the gold, I promise you I'll gloat. 'Till then I'll just pray. How about you, Barrie? I heard your chances just got better in floor exercise now that Vesely is out."

"Out?" Barrie blurted in complete surprise. "What do you mean? Why is she out?"

"You haven't heard? She's in the hospital. Word is she overdosed on something. They had to pump her stomach."

"Overdosed? No way. Not her. She has diabetes. She has to give herself shots all the time. We talked about it just the other day when I saw her giving herself one in the locker room. She said she hated it. It kind of freaked me out." Barrie's whole body trembled. "Just thinking about it now gives me the chills."

"Who is Vesely?" Samantha asked.

"Ivana Vesely. She's a Czechoslovakian gymnast. She's won like every floor exercise competition this year. She would have taken the gold without a doubt. I can't believe it. This is really gonna change things."

"How?" Samantha asked.

"With Vesely out, Xi-wei and Stefanya will probably take the gold and silver. There are about four of us who will now fight for the bronze."

"Who's Stefanya?" Samantha asked.

"A young Russian girl. She's really strong and filled with energy like a kid, but she has the poise and grace of an adult. The judges always love her. She's really great."

"And who are the others?"

"You heard me talk about Allie earlier?"

"Yup, one of your favorites."

Tony laughed. "One of her favorites, huh? That's pretty funny," he said.

Barrie smiled and nodded. "Yeah, well, she's one and there's also another Russian girl, Tatiana. And there's Yuuka. She's Japanese."

"That's it? Just three?" Samantha asked.

"You're looking at the fourth," Tony said.

Barrie smiled and shrugged her shoulders.

"Oh cool!" Chelsea said. "I'd love it if you won a medal."

"Yeah, me too!" Barrie giggled. "Hey, I want to get some sun and fresh air. Do you guys want to take a walk with me before I go back to practice?"

"Sure," Chelsea said.

"Tony, do you want to come?" Barrie asked.

"No, I have to head back to practice now. Will you girls be around later?"

Samantha and Chelsea looked at each other. Then they both looked at Barrie.

"You guys said you wanted to come back to the dorm and hang out with the team later, right?"

"Yeah," Samantha said.

"We can do it right after practice. Tony, can you come over and hang out for a while?"

"Sure. Sounds great."

"Okay, good. We'll see you later."

"Bye girls, nice to meet you," Tony said.

Samantha smiled and waved. "You too," she said.

Chelsea said, "See you later."

As they walked out the door, Samantha said, "He's cute! And what a body!"

"Yeah, he is cute," Barrie said. "We've been kind of dating on and off this past year. It's tough having a steady boyfriend while we're both competing. We're always traveling to different places."

"Yeah, I guess that would be tough."

"Yeah, it really stinks. It's one of the things I hate about competing at this level. That, and being away from my family so much of the time."

"I don't know if I could handle being away from my family all the time," Chelsea said.

"I got homesick a lot in the beginning. It still happens, but not as often anymore. Skype helps. I talk to my brother at college a lot and my parents and sister at home every day."

"What's Skype?" Samantha asked.

"It's a website that allows you to talk to anyone in the world for free as long as they have Skype too. It's really cool. You see each other as you talk."

"I gotta get that," Samantha said. "What's the site?"

"S-K-Y-"

Suddenly a thunderous blast stopped Barrie's spelling. The girls and everyone near them fell to the pavement. Something had exploded across the street. Debris crashed down around them. Lying prone, Samantha watched a small, twelve inch, inflated tire roll by. Then, she flinched as she saw the remnants of a big umbrella fall and hit a woman in the head, next to Barrie. The woman's scream was ear piercing.

"Are any of you hurt?"

Samantha turned to see Officer Camadeco kneeling next to Chelsea.

"Chelsea, are you alright?" Camadeco asked, touching Chelsea's arm.

Samantha turned and saw Barrie get up and pull some sticky debris from her tight, long, brown curls. "Eww," Barrie said, looking at her hair and smelling the gooey mess. "What the heck is this?"

"Are you okay?" Camadeco asked Chelsea, again.

Samantha turned to see Chelsea sitting on the street next to her and Camadeco.

"Yeah, I think I'm alright. My arm hurts. It's a little bloody."

Camadeco leaned closer to Chelsea and inspected a bleeding cut on her face. "You have a gash on your cheek too, but it doesn't look too bad." Camadeco looked over at Barrie and Samantha. "Are you two alright?"

Sirens were getting closer and much louder by the second.

"I think I'm okay," Samantha said.

"I'm alright, except for this junk in my hair." Barrie said. "It's not blood, is it?"

Camadeco stood and moved quickly to Barrie. She looked at her head. "I don't see any cuts." She took some of the sticky matter from Barrie's hair, rubbed it between her fingers and smelled it. "Vegemite!"

"Eww, that stuff is gross," Barrie groaned.

"At least it's not blood," Camadeco said. "I'm going to get a medic." She turned toward Chelsea, who was getting up. "Just sit where you are. I want you checked out and cleaned up."

Samantha looked around at the devastation. It looked a little like a war zone on TV. The woman who had been hit by the umbrella was being attended to by a medic. Besides her and Chelsea there didn't seem to be too many people who were hurt.

She turned when she heard Camadeco returning. "Here, this is her," she said to a young medic. "Please check the cuts on her face and arm. I think they're superficial but I want you to confirm it before she gets up."

"What was it? What exploded?" Samantha asked.

"A vending cart," Camadeco said.

"Was it a bomb?" Barrie asked.

"We don't know. The fuel tank exploded but we're not sure why yet. The vendor is nowhere to be found. It seems he left the scene before the explosion occurred."

"Oh my God! You think he was a terrorist?" Barrie asked.

"We're not sure, Barrie," Camadeco said.

Samantha flinched as Camadeco said Barrie's name.

Barrie's face scrunched up in curiosity. "How do you know my name?"

Camadeco glanced at Samantha and Chelsea, sighed, then said, "Barrie, I'm a police officer. I'm here on assignment. Let's all take a walk and I'll explain."

"Explain what?" Barrie asked. She looked at Samantha and Chelsea, neither had expressions of curiosity. "Wait, you guys know her?"

"Yup, we do and she's really cool," Samantha said. "Actually, she's assigned to watch us as we work here today."

"Huh? I don't get it. Why would you guys need police protection if you're just interviewing us for a story?"

"Let's wait for Chelsea to get cleaned up, then we'll take a walk and I'll explain it all," Camadeco said.

Samantha turned to Chelsea. The medic had cleaned and bandaged her face and arm. He confirmed the cuts were all superficial and that she had no other injuries.

"You're good to go, ma'am," the medic said. "Just make sure to clean those cuts daily with some antiseptic."

"Thank you," Chelsea said with a smile.

"My pleasure," he said as he stood. He looked at Samantha and Barrie. "Are you girls okay?"

"Yes, thanks," Samantha said.

"I could use some help getting up," Barrie said with a cute grin.

Samantha couldn't hold back a giggle as the medic helped Barrie to her feet.

"Thank you very much," Barrie said with a smile and a tiny flutter of her eyes.

Samantha laughed as the medic walked off, looking for someone else to help.

"What are you laughing at?" Barrie asked.

"Thank you very much," Samantha said batting her eyes, mimicking Barrie.

"Shut up! He was cute!" Barrie said.

"Yeah, he was," Chelsea agreed. "Really cute!"

"Okay, let's take that walk," Barrie said. "I really want to hear this explanation."

Samantha, Chelsea and Officer Camadeco all glanced at each other. Camadeco nodded and said, "Give me just a sec, Barrie. I need to speak with that officer over there." She nodded toward an officer near the smoldering remnants of the vending cart. "And I need to call my boss. I'll be right back. Samantha, will you come with me, please?"

"Sure."

**

Camadeco and Samantha sat in a nearby patrol car. Camadeco dialed the Chief and pressed the speaker button on the phone.

"Coyne here, go ahead," answered Chief Coyne.

"Chief, it's me, Donna. You heard about the explosion right?"

"I heard. How bad is it?"

"One fatality and one woman with a head injury, otherwise, only a few cuts and bruises. A lot of scared people, though."

"I'll bet. Napolitano is there, right?"

"Yeah, he seems to have things under control, at least, as much as possible."

"Good. How are you and the girls doing?"

"Chelsea got some superficial cuts on her face and arm. She'll be okay. The girls seemed to be doing a good job with the interviews, but I haven't had a chance to speak with them yet. Samantha is right here next to me. I brought her so she could tell you what she's learned so far."

"Okay. Very good."

Camadeco nodded to Samantha.

"Hi, Chief Coyne."

"Hi Samantha, how are the interviews going?"

"I think they're going well. Donna, oops, I mean Officer Camadeco." She glanced quickly over at Camadeco who made a face and mouthed, *don't worry about it.*

"Anyway, she gave us enough room that the girls didn't even know she was with us and it helped them loosen up. Some of them were very friendly and very talkative. We found out that Xi-wei, one of the top Chinese gymnasts and probable medalist in floor exercise has an interesting family history. Her parents were killed when she was little and she was raised by her aunt and uncle. Some of the things she said about her uncle seemed a little suspicious."

"Like what?" Chief Coyne asked.

"Well, her dad and her uncle had been partners in a construction business but she didn't know what they built. She said her aunt and uncle manage her gymnastics career and that her uncle had said that nothing but a gold medal would be acceptable. She must win it for her parents. She made him sound very demanding and very interested in the money that she'd earn. She also said that he is very private and that he always avoids reporters."

"That is interesting. Would you spell her name for me?"

"Sure, it's X I—W E I. We also heard about an American who's expected to medal in floor exercise. Allie Grecco. They said she's really mean and acts very entitled. Some of the girls think her dad is in the mafia."

"Really, did they say why?"

"No, not yet. But I'll ask. Oh yeah, I almost forgot, do you know about the Czechoslovakian gymnast who overdosed on something? I forgot her name but I wrote it somewhere and it's on my recorder."

"I know all about her, Samantha. Her name is Vesely, Ivana Vesely. It seems that she took the wrong medicine for her diabetes. I have someone interviewing her doctor now. Either he wrote the wrong prescription or it was filled incorrectly. We'll know more soon."

"You know she was the favorite for the gold, right?"

"Hm, I knew she was Czechoslovakia's best, but I didn't know she was favored for the gold. That's interesting. Good work, Samantha. Really good."

"Thank you, sir. Do you want the names of the other girls who are expected to win in floor exercise?"

"Yes, of course I do. Fire away."

Samantha dug through her notes. "Okay, this is what I was told. Now that Vesely is out, Xi-wei and Stefanya, a Russian girl, sorry but I don't have all the last names."

"That's okay, Samantha. We can get them easily. You're doing great."

"Okay, well, Xi-wei and Stefanya will probably take the gold and silver. Then there are four others who will most likely fight for the bronze. One is the American girl I mentioned before, Allie Grecco. Then, there's another Russian girl named Tatiana and Yuuka, a Japanese girl."

"That's three?" Coyne said.

"The fourth is Barrie Froehlich. She's actually the one who gave us most of this information. She knows Casey and Johnny very well from AllSport."

"Oh, really. Did she train there?"

"Yes, and she went to school there with the boys. They're friends."

"Hey Chief," interrupted Camadeco.

"Yes, Donna?"

"Barrie, the girl Samantha was just telling you about, is wondering why I am with the girls today. I had been watching them from a distance all day, but I had to check on them after the explosion. Barrie was with them and now she's curious about me. I was planning on telling her after we get off the phone with you. Is that alright?"

"Sounds like you don't have much choice. I think it's probably better that you explain the situation and convince her to remain quiet about it. Otherwise her curiosity will probably grow into suspicion, which will spread through the gymnastic community quickly."

"My thoughts exactly," Camadeco said.

"Alright you two, keep up the good work. I'll talk to you later."

Chapter 19

"THE ROOM IS empty," Jay said on the phone to Chief Coyne after searching the McCall's hotel room. "The beds don't even look like they were slept in last night. They left behind some make-up and some skin glue. The kind used for applying disguises."

"You think they left the hotel for good?" Coyne asked.

"Probably, but it's hard to say for sure. They may just be traveling very light. Living out of backpacks or something like that. They also left some burnt paper remnants that your forensics team is bringing back to the lab. I could only make out a few lines on the paper but it looked like it was probably a floor plan. I know Casey and the kids had said that when they saw them outside the other day at the gymnastics venue, she was studying plans of some type. The fact is, if they're targeting a female gymnast, there are only a few places that we need to cover. I was told the gymnasts don't go very far. They live and eat in their dorms, which are right near the gymnastics pavilion. Once in a while they go out to eat, and that's usually as a group. Chances are these people are planning to strike when the kid is alone."

"Right, that would be my guess too. You know what I also keep thinking?"

"What?" Jay asked.

"Maybe the drug problem with Vesely, the Czech girl, *was* the assassin's doing. Maybe they're *done* with their job and that's why they left. I mean the drug issue was quick and very effective. The world's top gymnast in floor exercise is now out of the competition. Samantha gave me a list of the girls who are now favored to win medals."

"Really, that's good."

"Very. A bunch of girls now have a chance who probably didn't before. Two girls are now favored for gold and silver. Four others are now in the running for the bronze."

"Did she get all their names?"

"She did better than that. She gave me names and also some questionable issues to dig into with parents and guardians."

"Like what?"

"One of the four American gymnasts now fighting for bronze is from Philadelphia. Many of the girls think her dad is connected."

"Mafia?"

"That's what they say."

"Hm, what's her name? I'll check it out."

"Allie Grecco," Coyne said.

"Grecco?" Jay repeated. "Give me a minute, I call you right back."

"Hold on, there's another. If you're going to call, might as well check both out."

"Another connected father? That seems strange."

"Yeah it does, but this one is Chinese. He's the uncle of Xiwei Mai. He's her guardian and her manager. Her parents died when she was a kid. Her aunt and uncle raised her and have been pushing her to win ever since. He's known to be very tough and very difficult to deal with within the gymnastics community."

"Samantha got all that?"

"No, I got a lot of it from Matt Marrow. Samantha got me the names and I called him to see what he or his staff knew about the girls."

"Alright, let me see what I can find out and I'll call you right back. You have all the dorms covered with your people, right?"

"Yes, but there are so many dorms, it's been kind of tough until now. Now that we know where to concentrate, I'll increase the size of the teams at the American, Russian and Chinese dorms. I also think it's time to warn the managers and coaches. If something is going to happen, it'll probably be before the Opening Ceremonies. There wouldn't be any reason for them to chance a hit during the Opening Ceremony or the competition. Their chances of getting caught would be much too high."

"Right," Jay said.

"Hey, you know about the explosion, right?"

"Explosion?"

"Yeah, I meant to tell you when we started this conversation. A vending cart outside the gymnastics pavilion blew up just a little while ago. Samantha, Chelsea and my officer were across the street."

"Oh no, are they okay?"

"Yeah. Chelsea got some minor cuts, but she'll be fine. There was one fatality. We're not sure if it was the vendor or not. The forensics team is at the scene now. They'll let me know as soon as they determine whether it was a bomb or an accident."

"You don't really think it was an accident, do you?"

"No, not really, but we have to check."

"This is all too coincidental."

"What do you mean?" Coyne asked.

"Well, if our friends moved out of here earlier and now we have an explosion just outside the gymnastics pavilion, my guess is that it was a diversion. Chief, the girls on that list need protection immediately! I just hope we're not too late. Get as many teams into that pavilion as you can. Get some sharpshooters on the roof and on top of all the surrounding buildings. Sorry if I sound like I'm giving you orders, but there's no time to be subtle right now."

"Forget subtle, mate. Just tell me what to do."

"I'm sure the bomb has already created enough chaos so that we don't have to work undercover anymore. Start a massive search of the area. Streets, buildings, anywhere your people feel that someone can hide or can take a shot from. Cover the dorms, the pavilion and everywhere between. I'm heading over now. I'll call you when I get there."

"Alright, see ya."

Chapter 20

"CAN WE LEAVE already? I'm tired of watching that idiot," Johnny said.

"Be nice, will you?" said Cindy.

"He's a jerk, Mom. He's mean to, like, everyone, but you."

"Well, you'll just have to wait. He's about to dive off the three meter and I want to see it. After that, we can go eat."

"Good, I'm starving," Johnny said.

"You're not starving and you know I hate when you say it," Cindy said. "There are lots of people in the world who are really starving. You might be hungry, but luckily you've never been starving."

Johnny rolled his eyes just like he did every time his mother gave him this lecture. Then, they all heard what sounded like a muffled explosion.

"What was that?" Shane asked.

"I'd say fireworks, but it's the middle of the day," Cindy said.

"Is there a construction site near here?" Johnny asked. "Maybe they're using dynamite."

"I don't think they'd allow construction anywhere near the Olympic grounds, do you?" Casey asked.

"Look, he's almost at the top," said Shane, nodding toward DeCappa.

Marco DeCappa climbed onto the platform and walked to the end. He turned around and slowly stepped his way backward to the edge. With the balls of his feet on the edge, and his heels off the platform, he raised his arms straight out to his sides. Then he looked straight ahead, lifted his arms up over his head and bounced slightly on the balls of his feet. He launched into an inward triple flip that looked perfect until he over-spun his entry, slapping the back of his legs hard on the water.

"Ouch," Shane said, as she and Cindy flinched and squirmed in their seats.

Johnny stood and coldly said, "Alright, let's get out of here."

"Johnny!" his mom said. "That's really rude."

Johnny shrugged. "Can we just get outta here?"

Cindy shook her head as she followed them all to the aisle and said, "I'll never understand how they can just climb up and do it again after hitting the water so hard."

"I know," Shane said. "It baffles me, too."

"At least they land in water," Casey said. "How about the sports where they land on snow or pavement?"

"I can't even watch those," Cindy said.

"It's really hard to believe that the wife of an ex Navy SEAL is such a wimp," Johnny said.

"That's why I married your father, Johnny. He's tough enough for both of us."

Johnny smiled and put his arm over his mother's shoulder as they walked down the steps and out the revolving door. They heard sirens and saw a speeding ambulance turn the corner across the far side of the plaza. They continued down the slate stairs, which ran the full width of the building, stepping around the throngs of tourists who were enjoying the sun and the hubbub of the Olympic Village. A rainbow of big colorful wigs bounced around on the heads of clowns on unicycles, who were juggling what looked like big Olympic rings in the center of the plaza down at street level.

Before they reached the bottom of the stairs, Shane said, "So where would you boys like to eat? Would you prefer a restaurant or should we get some sandwiches and eat right here on the steps?"

Johnny and Casey glanced at each other, then scoped around the plaza looking at the wide assortment of international restaurants. Casey slowly turned his head looking for something that sounded good. Everything from falafel to Jamaican beef patties was available within a one block radius. He quickly turned his head back, thinking he saw someone he knew. He was right. The beautiful Russian gymnast he saw yesterday was walking into a Greek restaurant. "How about Greek?" he said to the others.

"I wouldn't mind a Greek salad," Cindy said.

"Sounds good to me," Shane agreed.

"Cool, I love gyros!" Johnny said.

They made their way through the crowds to the entrance and Casey opened the door for them all. The hostess took their name and said the wait wouldn't be long.

"I'm going to go wait outside in the sun," Shane said. "Anyone want to come?"

"I will," Cindy said.

"Yeah sure," said Johnny.

"I'll wait here and come get you when they call us," Casey said.

"Oh, then I will too," Johnny said.

Casey smiled and nodded at Johnny.

"It smells so good in here," Johnny said. "I'm starving."

"You're *starving*?" Casey kidded with a grin.

"Oh, shut up."

They both laughed and Casey began looking around, scanning the restaurant, table by table.

"What are you looking for?" Johnny asked.

"Her," Casey said with a nod across the room.

"Who?" Johnny looked for a few seconds. "Oh, it's the Russian girl. What's her name?"

"Stefanya."

"She's so hot ... Wait, is that why you chose this place? How did you know she was here?"

"I saw her coming in when we were walking down the stairs."

The hostess approached them and said, "Your table is ready."

"Can you wait one second while we get our mothers? They're right outside."

"Of course."

Casey ran out, got Shane and Cindy, and they all followed the hostess to their table. Casey was a little disappointed that it was across the room from Stefanya, but at least she was in view.

Casey and Johnny picked up their menus and held them up in front of their faces. Casey held his at an angle that allowed him to view Stefanya from the side. Johnny lowered his just enough to peak over the top.

A waiter came by and placed a basket filled with piping hot pita bread wedges and a bowl of hummus in the middle of the table.

"Are you ready to order?" he said.

The women ordered their salads and Johnny ordered his gyro.

"I'll have the shish kabob, please," Casey said.

The waiter then took the menus and reached for Casey's.

"Can I look at it a little while longer?" he said.

"Sure, mate. No problem."

The waiter walked away and Casey put the menu back up in front of his face.

After a moment, Casey's mom asked, "Casey, what are you doing? Who are you looking at or hiding from?"

"He's looking at a Russian gymnast," Johnny said. "The girl over there. The one with the red hair." Johnny pointed in the girl's direction, but noticed something that made him flinch and look back toward Casey with wide eyes.

Casey looked at him. "What's the matter?"

"Uh. I, uh … I have to go to the bathroom." Johnny gave Casey a pleading look and mouthed, *come with me.*

Casey scrunched his face in curiosity and mouthed back, *what's wrong?*

Johnny's eyes were wide as he jerked his head in the direction of the bathroom and mouthed, *just come!*

"What's going on with you two?" Cindy asked.

"Nothing, we'll be right back," Casey said as he stood and tossed his napkin on the table next to his place setting. He was annoyed, but very curious. Following Johnny between tables to the back of the dining area, he said quietly, "What's up?"

Johnny raised a finger implying he wanted to wait a second. When they reached the small hallway that led to the restrooms, Johnny turned around with an intense look and said, "He's here!"

"You mean …" Casey stopped talking as a woman walked past them on her way to the ladies' room.

"Yeah, him," Johnny said.

"Oh my God! Where?"

"Don't look yet, but he's at a table between ours and hers. He's got a fake beard and moustache now."

"Is he with the woman?" Casey asked.

"I think he's alone."

Casey peaked around the corner of the hallway into the dining room. He studied the tables and stiffened up as soon as he saw the man. The guy was only a few tables away from where they were standing. Luckily, he was seated facing the front of the restaurant. Casey could see his profile very clearly. He looked at the dark beard and stared a moment just to make sure it was him. Then, he turned back toward Johnny. "You're right. I can't believe it. Stefanya must be his target, but why would he pick such a public place to do it?"

"I don't know. Maybe he was following her, waiting for the right moment and she ended up coming in here."

"Maybe."

"You think he'd try to kill her in here?"

"I don't know, but we can't take any chances. We have to do something right now!" Casey turned and looked again.

"Oh sure!" Johnny said. "A couple of teenagers are going to just walk over and stop an assassin."

"What's that?" Casey said, looking at the man.

"What's what?"

"He just took something out of his pocket." Casey saw what looked like a small bottle in the man's left hand and then, from the man's right hand Casey saw the glimmer of something tiny reflecting the bright fluorescent light from above. Casey watched intensely as the man lowered his hands to his lap and unscrewed the tiny bottle. Then he dipped the end of the shiny object in his right hand into the vial. Casey squinted to get a clearer view. It looked like some type of needle attached to a ring on the guy's middle finger.

Then the man quickly screwed the top back on the bottle and returned it to his pocket. He glanced around the room, and then stood.

"Oh my God, he's heading towards her." Casey turned quickly and looked down the bathroom hallway. "Hurry, go grab that folding chair and follow me!"

Johnny ran and grabbed the folded metal chair, and then ran back and caught up with Casey, who was already on his way towards the man. As Casey hurried past his place setting, he reached and grabbed the wooden handle of the metal shish-kabob skewer from his plate. A quick glance revealed about three inches of pointy metal protruding from the grilled lamb packed onto the skewer.

"Casey, what are you doing?" his mother asked, obviously concerned.

"Call Jay and call the police, right now, Mom!"

"*Why*," she asked nervously.

Casey didn't answer. Instead, he quickened his pace, shifting rapidly around a table of guests. Luckily, the restaurant was busy enough that waiters and guests caused adequate activity to conceal Casey and Johnny's pursuit. He quickly turned to Johnny and said, "I'm going around. You come up behind him and just be ready."

Johnny nodded with fear in his eyes.

Casey made another turn between tables and was now rapidly walking towards the man at an angle.

One more step and the man would be within reach of Stefanya. Casey had no time to plan; instead he jumped directly into the man's path and held up his skewer. "Don't even think about it!" Casey shouted fiercely.

The man flinched but didn't stop. He reached with his left hand and aggressively grabbed Casey's arm.

Suddenly Casey saw the metal chair come crashing down on the man's head with a sickening thud. The man fell sideways, bounced off a seated woman's shoulder and collapsed to the floor, unconscious. The woman and all those at her table screamed as he fell into her. People everywhere stood up trying to see what was happening. The entire restaurant instantly silenced. People seated close to the situation rapidly moved away. Stefanya ran to the far side of her table, but still had no idea that she had been in danger.

Johnny and Casey knelt down next to the man. Their hearts were racing, but they were too frightened to speak. Casey carefully reached for the man's right wrist and turned it so that his palm was facing up. Blood trickled from where the needle had pricked the man's palm. The needle was right there, connected to the ring Casey had seen earlier. A closer look at the man's finger under the ring revealed the small, dark line of a tattoo.

The loud sound of sirens filled the room as the front doors were opened by a group of police officers. Jay and Chief Coyne rushed in and then stopped quickly to evaluate the situation.

"Jay, over here, come quick," yelled Shane, who was now standing right behind Casey.

Jay and Coyne made their way quickly through the crowds. Coyne's hand was on his holstered handgun.

"Johnny," Casey said, trying to stay calm. "Go try to explain what happened to Stefanya. She still has no idea this was about her. Get a couple of the cops to stay with her."

As Johnny stood, his mom, now behind him, reached for his arm saying, "Honey, are you okay?"

"Yeah Mom, I'm fine. I'll be right back."

"Where are you going?"

"Just over there," he said, pointing toward Stefanya. "I need to go talk to her and get her protected." He moved away quickly just as Jay and Coyne arrived by Casey's side.

Jay knelt down next to Casey. "Are you alright?"

"Yeah, scared, but okay. I think."

"What about him?"

"I can't tell, Jay. I think he may be dead. Oh my God." Casey put his hands up and covered his heart. "I don't feel so good. It's hard to breathe."

"Okay, everyone get back, please give us some room." Jay took Casey's arm. "Come on, son, let's get you some fresh air." Jay turned toward Shane. "Take him outside. I'll be there in a minute." Jay turned to an officer. "Officer, please stay with them until I come out."

The officer nodded and led the way, parting the crowd as Casey and Shane followed.

Casey was a few steps away when he turned back and said, "Jay, be careful. He has a needle in his right hand. He was going to poison her."

The crowd around him gasped at his statement. They still had no idea why the whole situation had occurred. As far as most of the guests were concerned, it had looked like two young kids had just killed an innocent man.

"Poison who?" Jay asked.

"Stefanya, the redhead with Johnny." Casey nodded his head in their direction. She was talking to Johnny with two officers next to them.

"Thanks Casey," Jay said. "Good work. Go on out and get some fresh air."

Casey turned and the officer led them out.

"Johnny," Jay said loudly enough to get his attention.

Johnny stopped speaking and looked over at Jay.

"Where's the woman?" Jay said loudly. "Was she with him?"

Johnny shook his head.

Jay closed his eyes for a moment and sighed, then knelt down next to Coyne.

"He barely has a pulse," Coyne said. "Watch that hand, I think he stuck himself with the poisoned needle when he fell. Whatever poison or drug he used seems to be killing him very slowly."

"He deserves it, but I wish we could just speak with him." Jay shook his head in disgust.

Coyne looked at Jay. "What's the matter, mate?"

"The woman. The boys say she wasn't with him. We're not done yet."

Now it was Chief Coyne's turn to sigh.

Officers had cleared a wide path through the crowd to allow the medics, who had just arrived, to wheel in a gurney. The first medic to reach them said, "Sorry we took so long, mate. The first ambulance had a bit of an issue."

"What kind of issue?" Coyne asked.

"They hit a woman on a motorcycle at an intersection about a block from here."

Coyne and Jay looked at each other. "You don't think?" Jay said.

"It could be," said Coyne. "Maybe she was waiting for this clown and she took off when she heard all the sirens coming." He looked at the medic. "Is she alive?"

"Yeah, I heard them on the radio talking about a possible concussion and some cuts and bruises. They said her helmet and motorcycle leathers saved her from getting really ripped up."

"You didn't see her, did you?" Jay asked.

"No, why?"

"Because we need to know if she's this guy's accomplice." Jay pointed at the man on the floor. "Is she conscious?"

"You want me to check right now or do you want me to save this guy first?" The medic had knelt down while he was talking and was feeling the man's neck. "If you want to keep him alive, we need to get him out of here right away."

"You and your partner can load him onto the gurney and then one of my officers will help wheel him out while you check on the woman. Be careful though, the ring on his right hand has a poisoned needle attached to it. Instead of pricking his target, he stuck himself with it as he fell."

"His target?" the medic said as they hoisted the man onto the gurney.

"Yes, he's an assassin."

"You're pulling my leg, right mate?" The medic slowly turned the man's right hand over to look. "Crickey! Would you look at that!" He looked at the other medic. "Hey, ya see this, mate? Be careful, the whacker's got a poisoned needle in his right hand. Don't touch it!"

"We're going to need that." Coyne turned to one of his men. "Charlie, help him wheel this out and get the ring off the guy's finger and into an evidence bag."

The officer nodded and helped push the gurney out.

"Okay," Coyne said to the medic. "Call your bloke at the hospital now. We need to find out about the woman."

The medic pulled his two-way radio from his belt, lifted it to his mouth, and pushed the button. "Steve to Karen, come in." He waited a moment for an answer but received nothing. "Karen Moore, please come in."

"Steve, this is dispatch. We're in the middle of a crisis at the moment. What do you need?"

"I'm with officer, uh?" The medic looked at Coyne and raised his eyebrows.

"Coyne, Chief Coyne."

"I'm here at the Greek restaurant. We're loading the patient in the wagon. It's police business and Chief Coyne wants to ask some questions about that woman motorcycle rider who hit Karen's rig. Are they at the hospital?"

"Police business? Well, that explains it."

"Explains what?" the medic asked.

"They were on their way to the hospital and the woman pulled out a gun. She's just taken Karen and Ron hostage."

Coyne reached for the medic's radio. "Dispatch, this is Chief Coyne. Did you report this to the police yet?"

"No, Chief. It just happened a minute ago. I was about to call it in when I heard Steve radioing Karen."

"Okay, where is the ambulance right now?"

"Heading southeast on Parramatta Road. It's just crossing Homebush Bay Drive."

"Good, I take it you're following them on your computer?"

"Yes, Chief. I follow all the rigs within our dispatch area."

"Okay, I'm handing the radio over to Jay Scott. I want you to keep him informed and follow his orders. I'm going to get patrol cars there now."

"Roger, Chief."

Coyne handed the medic's radio to Jay, and then pulled his police radio from his belt and raised it to his mouth. "Coyne here, I want all patrol cars in the vicinity of Parramatta and Homebush Bay Drive to listen up. We have a hostage situation inside an ambulance. The vehicle is heading southeast on Parramatta. Close in on the ambulance and await your orders. Who is close right now?"

"512 Chief. Four blocks out and closing in."

"504 here. We are two blocks away."

"565 Chief. Heading northwest now on Parramatta. Ambulance should be within sight any second. Okay, there it is."

"528 checking in. We're about fifteen blocks south and heading north."

"504 here. Ambulance in sight."

"Good, follow it and wait for my orders. Everyone else, check in when you have the vehicle in sight."

"Roger that."

"10-4 Chief."

Still speaking into his police radio, he said, "Coyne to dispatch."

"Dispatch here."

"You've been listening, right?"

"Of course, Chief."

"I want all the responding cars to be able to hear the ambulance dispatcher and the driver on our radios. Can you make that happen?"

"Sure, Chief. Use their radio and ask the dispatcher what channel they're using. It's probably fifty-two."

Coyne looked at Jay, who was already asking the ambulance dispatcher the question. The dispatcher confirmed that they were on channel fifty-two.

"All responding patrol cars, switch your vehicle radios to channel fifty-two so you can listen in to the ambulance driver and her dispatcher. Use your mobile radios to communicate with me. Everyone got that?"

"Loud and clear, Chief."

"Good," Coyne said. "Patrol car 504, check in."

"504 checking in."

"512 check in."

"Drive faster," a woman's voice blasted over the radio.

"Who was that?" Coyne asked.

"That's the woman in the ambulance, Chief," said the ambulance dispatcher. "It seems that Karen, the driver, locked the button on her radio in talk mode. We can hear everything in the rig."

"Good," Coyne said. "512, 528 and 565 check in."

"565 checking in."

"512 checking in."

"528 checking in."

"Where do you want me to go?" asked the ambulance driver.

"I want a helicopter," the woman said. "Get your dispatcher to call the police and tell them to get me a chopper."

"Dispatch, are you there?"

"Yes, Karen."

"Please call the police and tell them we need a helicopter."

Coyne and Jay looked at each other. They were impressed that the driver was staying so calm.

"Not a police chopper," the woman demanded. "Make sure it's civilian."

"Dispatch, make that a civilian helicopter, please."

"I'm speaking with the police now," The dispatcher said. "Where do you want the chopper?"

"Where's the closest place it can land?" the woman asked.

"The closest helipad is about twenty minutes from here," Karen said.

"Too long," the woman said. "There has to be something closer. A park, a parking lot, anything."

"Have them land on the fairway of the eighteenth hole at Concord Golf Club," Karen told the dispatcher.

"Good thinking," the woman said. "Tell her I want it fully fueled and I only want one pilot aboard. I don't want anyone else on board or anywhere within view of our path from the ambulance to the chopper."

"*Our* path?" Karen asked in a concerned voice.

"Yes, *you're* my new insurance policy."

"Oh, wonderful," Karen mumbled. "So, where are we going? Someplace fun, I hope."

"Tell you what, if you help me get on that helicopter and if I escape this mess, I will wire you enough money that you'll be able to take a few years off and live anywhere in the world you want."

"Hm, that sounds great, but could I ask you a favor?"

"What?"

"Could you pull that gun away from my head? I'm trying to stay calm and do what you want, but every time I look in my rear-view mirror and see that thing inches from my head, it makes me a little nervous."

"How far are we away from the golf course?"

"A few minutes."

"Ask your dispatcher when the chopper will be there."

Karen picked up the radio and said, "Dispatch, do we have an ETA for the helicopter?"

"I was told ten minutes, but a few minutes have gone by already."

Chief Coyne, Jay and everybody in the patrol cars could hear everything in the ambulance and still communicate with each other, without those in the ambulance hearing them.

"I can't believe that driver is keeping her head together," Jay said.

"I know her," said the officer standing next to them. "Chief, she's Frank Secret's sister."

"Well, that explains it," Coyne said. "She comes from a family of police. Her brother, her sister, and her father are all cops and her grandfather was one, too."

Jay nodded. "That's good. So, how well do you know this golf course that she's headed to?"

"Pretty well. We hold our annual police tournament there."

"Do the officers you sent earlier have high powered rifles in their cars?"

Coyne nodded. "Yeah." He raised his police radio to his mouth and pushed the talk button. "Carpenter, Sanborn come in."

Both officers checked in.

"Are you both at the course?"

"Yes, Chief. There are four of us here."

"Okay, you guys decide who the two best marksmen are. One should probably go to the roof of the clubhouse or wherever you have a clear shot to the fairway. You guys pick the other spot. We'll have to hope the ambulance driver parks far enough from the chopper to give us a decent chance to take the woman out. Did you guys hear that the driver is Frank Secret's sister?"

"Yeah, we heard, Chief. Tommy here is friends with her. He said she's tough as nails."

"Just like the rest of her family," Coyne said. "Let's just make sure she stays that way."

"10-4, Chief."

"Alright. Take your positions; they should be there any minute. Good luck guys. Out."

"How long should it take us to get there?" Jay asked.

"About ten minutes. Why?"

"Because we need to find out who's behind all this. Whoever it is needs to pay. Sorry if it sounds like I'm taking it personally, but when someone puts a hit out on kids, it just doesn't sit well with me. Hopefully the guy will live, but I don't think we're going to get to talk to him anytime soon, so I'd like a chance to speak with the woman."

"Don't tell me you don't want my guys to take her out."

"No, I wouldn't chance the life of the medic. I'm just hoping we get lucky."

"Well then, let's get out of here."

They ran out of the restaurant and saw Casey, Johnny, their mothers, Stefanya and a couple of officers standing together. Jay approached them saying, "We have to run. I'll meet you back at the hotel as soon as I can."

"Where are you going?" Casey asked.

"I want to question the woman, but we have to rush."

"So, we got her?" Johnny asked excitedly.

"Well, not yet. But we should any minute."

"I want to come," Casey said.

"Enough already, Casey. *No way!*" his mother said.

"Casey, you and Johnny have done enough. You both just saved her life." Jay nodded towards Stefanya. "And you risked your own lives to do it. You guys are heroes! Now, do me and your parents a favor. Go back to the hotel and just sit by the pool for the rest of the day. You still have a head injury and you need to rest. I'll be there as soon as I can and I'll explain whatever we find out."

"Fine," Casey said, sullenly.

Jay and Coyne sprinted to Coyne's car and took off with the lights flashing and sirens blasting.

Chapter 21

"THERE IT IS," Karen said, driving fast.

"The golf course? Where?" the woman asked, still holding her gun too close to Karen's head.

"No, the helicopter. It's coming down over there. That's where the golf course is."

"Hurry!"

"Move the gun and I'll hurry."

"You really are feisty, aren't you?"

"Not so much. But I grew up in a family of cops. I'm used to guns. Maybe not pointed at my head, but I'm used to them being around. I thought about being a cop, but I like this better. Until today, anyway!"

"If I take the gun away, are you gonna keep driving to the helicopter?"

"If I don't, you're going to shoot me, right?"

"Yeah."

"I don't have much choice then, do I?"

"Feisty and smart. I like that."

"A lot of good it's doing me right now."

"Is that the entrance, right up there?"

"Yup."

"Okay, call your dispatcher and tell her to call the police again. If any of those patrol cars behind us follow us through the entrance, you're dead."

"Gee, thanks."

"Just do it."

Karen did as she was told, then she drove the ambulance through the gated entrance and up a long driveway to the parking lot.

"Where's the chopper?" the woman asked anxiously.

"Through those trees, on the fairway. You'll see it in a second."

"Okay, when you pull up to it, I want you to get as close as possible and park the ambulance with the back door facing the chopper. Okay?"

Karen didn't respond.

"I said, okay?" the woman demanded.

"Yes, fine. Stop yelling. I'm nervous enough already."

"C'mon, drive faster. Hurry up."

Karen turned to her colleague, Ron, who had been sitting in the passenger seat the whole time. He was pale as a ghost, drenched in sweat and his eyes were closed tightly.

"There it is. See it?" Karen said to the woman, hoping it would get Ron to open his eyes. Then, hoping the woman was distracted, Karen turned to Ron, who looked at her with sickening fear in his eyes. Karen mouthed *hold on*, as she made a show of lifting her hand from the wheel and clenching it on the stationary handle on the door. He looked at her questioningly, so she let go and re-gripped the handle, making sure he saw her tighten her grip. She sighed as she finally saw him subtly brace himself.

"Remember, don't stop until the truck is close to the helicopter."

Karen sped up and drove off the pavement onto the damp grass. They only had about fifty meters to go to reach the helicopter. First, she had to drive through a row of huge oak trees to get to the fairway. The trees were about four meters apart, more than enough room to fit the ambulance easily through. As the ambulance began bouncing on the bumpy turf, Karen stepped harder on the gas pedal. As the vehicle sped up, she glanced into the rearview mirror just in time to see the woman take a quick step back and try to grab the shelves to steady herself. They were about three meters from the trees when all of a sudden Karen spun the steering wheel hard and simultaneously stomped on the brake pedal. The truck went into a sideways skid and slammed into one of the trees. The force of the crash threw the woman head first into the wall of the ambulance, leaving her dazed and ripping the gun from her hand.

Supercharged with adrenalin, Karen popped off her seat belt and sprang from her chair. She jumped into the back, searched the inside of the vehicle and spotted the gun. Not knowing the woman's condition, Karen lunged for the pistol, picked it up and quickly aimed it at the dazed assassin's head.

"How do you feel now, being on the other end of the barrel?" she said anxiously through gritted teeth.

Ron managed to open his door and roll out of the vehicle, dropping to the grass.

The officers waiting in the cars at the gate had heard the loud crash and drove as fast as possible, each skidding to a stop on the grass, near the ambulance. They ran and quickly pulled the back doors of the ambulance open to see Karen standing there, pointing the gun at the woman.

"Okay Karen, we've got it now," an officer said. "Give me the gun."

Karen slowly turned and handed the pistol to the officer, who had his own gun in his other hand, pointed at the woman. She was alive and conscious, but unable to move.

Another officer helped Karen out of the ambulance and down the step. All her energy suddenly seemed to leave her at once and she collapsed into the officer's arms.

Jay and Chief Coyne arrived at the scene moments later. They walked over to Karen, who was now sitting on a bench sipping from a bottle of water.

"Karen, I'm Chief Coyne. Are you okay?"

"Yes, Chief, I think so. Thanks."

"I want to commend you on how you handled this whole situation. You did as good, if not better, than any of my officers could have. You've really done your family proud, which I know isn't easy."

Karen laughed. "Yeah, I come from a tough bunch. Don't I?"

"That's for sure," Coyne said, now looking around. "You stay here and rest. We need to go speak with the woman. I'll give you a ride home when we're done."

"That's okay, Chief. They told me that my brother is on his way."

"Okay, good. Where is the woman?" he asked another officer, who was standing close by.

"Still in the ambulance, Chief. They cuffed her to the gurney and found this when they searched her." He handed Chief Coyne a black plastic remote clicker with a small red button on it.

"The remote she used to trigger the bomb on the vending cart," Jay said.

Coyne nodded and he and Jay walked away towards the ambulance.

Chapter 22

HOURS LATER, ON the big, slate patio surrounding the hotel swimming pool, a small crowd had formed. At the center, Casey and Johnny were explaining the earlier events of the day to their fathers, Samantha, Chelsea, and to some of the undercover officers who had been stationed at the hotel.

Just as Chief Coyne and Jay walked over, they heard Reid Clark exclaim, "Shish Kabob? You threatened an assassin with a shish-kabob skewer?"

The crowd laughed along with Casey and Johnny.

"Whatever, Dad. I had to improvise and it worked just long enough for Johnny to hit the guy over the head with a folding chair."

"That had to hurt," Johnny's dad said.

"You guys never cease to amaze me," said Stu, Reid's other body guard. "You always seem to be in the right place at the right time. First, you overhear these clowns down in the gym. Then, you see them the other day at the gymnastics pavilion. Then today, you stop the guy from killing one of the best gymnasts in the world."

"Yeah, with shish-kabob and a folding chair," Joel said, laughing again.

"Hey guys, let's not forget to mention our newest additions to the Junior Sports Sleuth Club," Jay added. "Let's hear it for our undercover reporters, Samantha and Chelsea. They managed to get information from the gymnasts that will now help us get to the bottom of this whole case."

"Yeah, that and the fact that they survived a vegemite explosion," added Casey, creating another round of laughter.

As the laughter subsided, Casey continued, "So, Uncle Jay, tell us what happened with the woman. We know you got her, but how?"

Jay and Chief Coyne described the chase, the accident and the expertise that Karen, the ambulance driver, handled it all with.

"So, tell us, did the woman talk?" Johnny asked.

"Yes, we got it all," Jay said. "Samantha and Chelsea were right. Xi-wei's uncle had set everything up. He's very wealthy and although it doesn't look like he's mobbed up, he is very corrupt and has friends in the Triad. He wanted Xi-wei to win so badly that he had his people hire the assassins to take out Stefanya. He's also responsible for the issue with the Czech girl's diabetes medication. We're not sure yet whether he paid off the doctor or the pharmacist to give her the wrong medication. There are many people who are going to end up in jail all around the world due to this incident, thanks to you four kids. You guys have not only saved lives, you have also made sure that the Opening Ceremonies and the Olympic Games will be safe for the world." The crowd surrounding them had grown large and after Jay's statement, everyone was applauding for Casey, Johnny, Samantha and Chelsea.

Chief Coyne asked the crowd for quiet and proceeded to explain that the World Olympic Committee and the Australian Olympic Committee were preparing a ceremony that would take place after the games were over to honor the kids and Karen, the ambulance driver.

Applause once again broke out throughout the gathered crowd. This time a bunch of the teens who were in the crowd of guests got together, picked up the four kids and launched them, laughing and screaming happily into the pool.

Reid stood and said, "May I have your attention, folks? Since most of this happened while I was on the golf course, I really had no idea that my son and his friends had put their lives on the line to help save others today. I must say that I am thrilled and filled with pride, but not at all surprised by their actions. Obviously, I am very happy that everything worked out as it did. To honor the kids and their amazing accomplishment and to celebrate a safe and enjoyable Olympic Games, please join us for ice cream sundaes for everyone." The doors to the hotel opened and waiters wheeled out four ice cream carts with all the makings for sundaes.

Everyone around the pool enjoyed the ice cream party and the laughter continued as Casey and Johnny together threw all four of their parents into the pool. Then, they both jumped in as well and gave their parents wet hugs.

Casey turned to Johnny and held out his fists. Johnny balled his fists and gave Casey a knuckle tap. "We did it," Casey said. "We solved another one."

"We sure did!" Johnny said with a wet smile.

Michael Balkind's novels Sudden Death and Dead Ball are en-
dorsed by literary greats including James Patterson, Clive Cussler,
John Lescroart, Wendy Corsi Staub and Tim Green. He has
appeared on ESPN's The Pulse, Sportsnet's Daily News Live, and
has co-hosted The Clubhouse radio show. He is a member of
Mystery Writers of America. Balkind's next novel, The Fix, is co-
authored with NBC Sports and Golf Channel Host, Ryan Burr.
Balkind graduated from Syracuse University and resides in New
York.

Balkind's website: www.balkindbooks.com
His author page on Facebook:
Michael Balkind—Mysteries & More
Follow him on Twitter: @michaelbalkind

CPSIA information can be obtained at www.ICGtesting.com
Printed in the USA
BVOW03s0452100415

395604BV00001B/7/P